Bird *with* Expanded Wings

by *SportyMan*

This is a work of fiction. Names, characters, places, and incidents are a product of the author's imagination. Locales and public names are sometimes used for atmospheric purposes. Any resemblance to actual people, living or dead, or to businesses, companies, events, institutions, or locales is completely coincidental.

Cover design by Bob Hurley (hurley.bob@hotmail.com)

Bird with Expanded Wings/SportyMan. -- 1st ed.
ISBN 978-0-578-65941-1

1

James walked deliberately into a Manhattan women's' consignment shop. He was a well-groomed and comfortably dressed man about the age 40, and he proceeded with confidence and purposeful demeanor. He didn't even glance at the used clothing but rather walked directly to a female salesperson. He was greeted by a warm voice.

"May I help you find anything in particular?"

She was dressed conservatively and generated more professionalism than sincerity and appeared to be in her early to mid-forties. Her short hair and extremely slender frame characterized a plain woman, certainly not a raving beauty. It was impossible not to notice that her left eye did not move as she focused on James's face. It was less obvious that her left arm was also severely handicapped.

"Yes, you may. I am intent on speaking with Connie Taylor".

She was struck by his formality and choice of words and responded: "I am Connie Taylor".

He reached inside his jacket pocket and said: "I have an envelope for you" and handed it to her while maintaining his deliberate manner. His demeanor suggested to Connie that it must be some kind of a legal document. To the contrary, she was overwhelmed to discover a cashier's check for $264,000.00. Seconds later, she recovered and asked: "<u>WHAT</u> is this? Some kind of joke or scam?" Her voice was indignant.

"It is not a joke. It is child support payments for the past 22 years."

Tearfully, she responded: "<u>WHO</u> are you and <u>WHY</u> are you giving me this money"?

"I am your son's father."

"You are <u>not</u> Robert Young!"

"I was 22 years ago when I abandoned you. Now I am James Whitmore. I received word that a hitman had a bullet aimed at ending my life. I couldn't take the chance of you and the child being harmed, and I fled the country".

"I don't believe you: Your appearance couldn't have changed that drastically."

"I had plastic surgery immediately when I arrived in China". My estranged father lived there and arranged it."

"I thought your father lived in Chicago?"

"Connie, I told you a lot of make-believes to protect my true life. I was not a government security guard. I was an FBI undercover agent investigating money-laundering. My suspect discovered my motives and arranged to make me extinct".

"So, everything you told me was a lie?"

"Not everything. I told you that I was in love with you and that was the absolute truth. Our short time together was the best of my life.

"Maybe this money is also a lie?"

"Connie, did Robert Young have a birth mark?"

She paused and responded: "Yes."

"Look at the back of my neck."

She pulled his shirt collar down and viewed what she remembered so well. She felt shivers looking at the small bird with wings expanded.

Then she blurted out: "DO you have any idea what my life has been like as a poor, single mother? Raising a son who has been embittered most of his life because his father abandoned him. Worrying every day that his gang life will get him killed. Not knowing where he is for weeks at a time."

"Connie, I know I don't deserve to be part of your lives, but I am here now and want to help. I need to help to feel worthy and, perhaps, save my soul. This is the physical body you have despised for 22 years, and I don't expect you to forgive me. I know I misled you and caused much grief. Let me walk you to the bank to deposit that cashier's check. It is like cash and needs to be deposited immediately. I have watched you make store deposits at the Bank of America across the street, and I drew that check at that bank just before walking in here. They will confirm its authenticity."

"How did you get this money?" she queried in a non-aggressive inquiring manner.

"I sold my father's new-car dealership and came back to the U.S. two months ago and have been observing your life. If you were happily married and financially secure, I would not be asking for this chance to redeem myself. I observed Robert, Jr. visiting at your apartment and his participation with the street gang. Your concern is warranted: "He needs to change directions quickly before he runs afoul of the law. I have some resources that will help me curtail his perilous lifestyle. I don't want him to know that I am his father until his life is changed. The bitterness and negative attitude he exhibits would only magnify if his good-for-nothing father surfaced."

2

As they walked to the bank, Connie, still skeptical, needed more answers.

"Why did you wait 22 years to reappear? Why so long? I needed help a long time ago and nearly died from the stress you caused. I eased my sorrow by convincing myself that you had been killed in an accident rather than believing that you left us to struggle and survive on our own."

"I couldn't contact you, even with money, as the risk of connecting me to you was too great. The man I was investigating was too powerful, and I had witnessed his crimes of greed and torture. Had he known of our connection, he would have used you and Robert, Jr. to bring me out of hiding. I got word from the FBI that he was murdered seven months ago. It wasn't until then that I felt safe to contact you. My FBI contact located you. They owed me that and still owe me for 22 years of hiding."

Connie listened intently and then asked: "How did you reconnect with your father?"

"I knew where he was since I joined the FBI right out of college. He had left the country when I was 8 years old and sent my mother money on a regular basis. He owed the IRS a lot of money as he refused to pay taxes. Finally, his debt forced him to leave. I had no interest in contacting him until I needed a place to hide. He was financially well-off and very pleased that I needed his help. I worked in his legitimate car dealership and managed the business until he had a heart attack three years ago. It took two years to find a buyer. I wanted to be liquid and financially able to return to the U.S. and help you when it became possible. The money-launderer went to prison with the evidence I produced. One of his criminal enemies had him murdered when he was released from prison. Apparently, he provided evidence in order to shorten his imprisonment."

A light snow was falling as they crossed Madison Avenue and the planted trees were shimmering in the sunlight. Connie felt like she was entering a new life. Her tired body was increasingly energized. Her left dangling arm was irrelevant and, for the first time since her stroke 8 years ago, she was unaware of her stressful life. She was glad to be alive. The euphoric sensation generated her meditative silence, even though she had many more questions for this stranger who was asking to be part of her life. She wasn't at all sure that she would permit that. However, "being rich" provided many options. How would the money change her life? Would she keep her store? Would she move to the country and try to take Robert, Jr. off the deadly streets? Would she go back to school: something she had wanted to do for a very long time? What would she study? All of these thoughts crossed her racing mind before they entered the bank.

James was holding her right elbow at they crossed the street. He intuitively felt that she needed assistance even though he had observed her self-sufficiency for two months. Helping her generated his feelings of worthiness. A longing that momentarily evaporated. He wondered if Connie would let him attempt to repair the damage. She was asking questions and he assessed them as a positive sign of her consideration. Unless he had her approval, he wouldn't approach Robert, Jr. He didn't feel he had the moral right to interfere in her life. However, he desperately needed her acceptance of his offer. He knew she would need time, and he wasn't going to pressure her. The questions, if they kept coming, would give him the opportunity to let her decide in his favor. His optimism was unchanneled, and he realized that he must control his enthusiasm in order to prevent the risk of assuming too much. Her initial reaction was encouraging: that was enough for now.

The bank teller gladly opened a savings account in the name of Connie Taylor, a single woman.

She immediately spoke: "I need to get back to the shop, and I have a lot to think about."

James replied: "Can I have dinner with you this evening?"

Connie paused and then replied: "I need to think about all of this. Not tonight, perhaps tomorrow."

Connie knew she wanted to talk to her best friend over a glass of wine to "air out" her thoughts. Her intuition was screaming to her to separate herself from this "ex-lover stranger" immediately. Right now, she didn't want to hear another word and wasn't certain that she ever would. It was too surreal, too overwhelming, and even created feelings of fear. She was confused as only minutes earlier she had felt euphoric crossing the street with that check. She questioned her intuition and didn't understand her fear: "Now I am rich. What is there to be afraid of?" she asked herself silently.

3

Without expressing any sentiment, she bid Robert, if he was Robert, goodbye and returned to her small shop. It was 3 p.m. and she told her friend and employee, Alice, that she was closing the shop early.

Alice asked why and remarked: "You are pale. Who was that man?"

Connie wasn't able to reply honestly and only responded: "An old acquaintance".

Alice was still concerned and further asked: "Did he tell you something that frightened you? Your voice is weak and frail."

Connie was momentarily introspective as she was uncomfortable misleading her good friend. However, she wasn't able to talk about the last half hour.

"Nothing to be concerned about, in fact he brought good news. I just need some time to digest it. I will tell you about him later."

As she said it, she wasn't at all certain that she would ever be able to tell her that he was Robert, Jr.'s father. At that instant, she understood her fear: maybe it was gang money that Robert, Jr. was hiding. He always seemed to have lots of money and had offered it to her often. However, she wouldn't accept it knowing that he didn't have a job and suspecting that the money was illegal. Perhaps this stranger was part of the gang but how would he know about the birthmark? The only person she ever told about that birth mark was Evelyn, her best friend since right after high school. As young girls, they often talked about their romances, few as they were. Connie remembered telling her when Robert gave her an orgasm, she always stroked the bird's wings and became the bird during climax. She wondered if Evelyn remembered the sensation she had revealed. Connie could still remember it vividly. She had experienced sexual satisfaction with three other men since Robert and the flying bird freedom had not occurred. Although very enjoyable, she had remained grounded every time. Robert was her first lover when she was a senior in high school. He was four years older and had experience. They had been dating for six months when the French-kissing escalated to lightly biting her nipples. Two dates later, his hand massaged her vagina and she didn't stop him as it felt wonderful. She could feel his hard penis when he pressed against her, and she wanted to caress it. On the night he put her hand inside his boxer shorts, he came quickly, and she felt like a woman, having fulfilled his masculine desire. He groaned as he came, and her wet hand confirmed his satisfaction. It was an easy decision for her to pleasure him on each date, and two months later, she was pregnant. The first time the bird flew, she was sitting on a bed in a motel room and he was giving her oral sex with his French-kissing tongue. She always stroked his neck after that first time.

Evelyn had been aghast when she heard Connie's experience. She was also astonished when Connie told her she was pregnant. Three months later, she was devastated when Robert evaporated from Connie's life.

Connie eagerly wanted to share today's revelation and hear Evelyn's reaction.

Connie phoned Evelyn from the shop and asked if she could come over as she had news to tell her.

Evelyn quickly confirmed her availability as the word "news" was exciting. She had been divorced three years earlier and relied on Connie's friendship to regularly uplift her spirits. She respected Connie's stamina knowing that Connie's life had been more difficult that her own. She often said to herself: "If Connie can make it, surely I can". Her two adult children quite often asked her for money, which she didn't have. She worked at a hair salon and barely earned enough to provide the necessities to survive and was continually hoping to find a boyfriend who would provide a better life. Thus far, all the men she had dated were failing candidates. She was attractive with an appetizing body and dated often. Although quite often enjoying good sex, usually a maximum of two dates provided enough information to qualify a failed prospect: not needing "a rich guy", just one who earned a "good living" and would pay her rent. The few who could afford to pay her rent only wanted her body, not a commitment. She hadn't given up hope, but the search was wearisome: sharing the details of her disappointments with Connie at each visit. They drank a lot of cheap wine and sometimes slept over as they had overindulged. She felt their friendship couldn't be any closer, even though Connie often told her she shouldn't be sleeping with so many guys. Responding, by offering that she couldn't afford vacations and would enjoy pleasure when she had the opportunity.

4

Connie arrived exhibiting more energy than normal, and Evelyn knew her excitement about news was warranted.

"What is it? What is it?" she queried. "Well, I had a visitor at the shop today."

"And go on?"

"He had a birthmark on the back of his neck."

"What do you mean? What kind of mark? Not a bird?"

"Yes, a bird with expanded wings."

"You mean Robert is alive?"

"I mean he says he is Robert, but I don't know if I can believe him."

"Where has he been? And why did he come back?"

Connie told her Robert's story and then said, "I haven't told you the best news yet: He gave me a check for $264,000.00. I am a rich woman."

Evelyn was speechless. It was probably sixty seconds before she said: "It has to be Robert. Why would anyone else give you all that money?"

Connie expressed her concern of illegal money, and Evelyn replied: "Don't look a gift horse in the teeth to see how old he is, just ride him out as that is his wish. You deserve the money, just accept that it is legal and don't manufacture concerns. When are you going to see Robert again?"

"I didn't tell him I would."

"Connie, you must. You don't owe him any time, but you owe yourself answers. Where is he staying?"

"I don't know but I am sure he will contact me for my answer."

"Connie, you have nothing to lose by accepting his offer to help Robert, Jr. You worry about him continuously and, with help, you will know more about his life on the streets. Robert obviously has contacts that can provide information that you will otherwise never know. I am not a religious person, but this is a "Godsend" miracle opportunity. Did Robert talk at all about your relationship when you were 18?"

"He told me that he was in love with me then, and it was the best part of his life."

"For goodness sakes, girl, that should make you feel pure. Your son was conceived out of love, not deceit as you have always expressed."

"Evelyn, did you ever tell anyone about Robert's birthmark?"

Evelyn hesitated with an expression of dismay and said: "Yes, a number of people but I never mentioned any names. I told some girlfriends about your flight sensation during orgasm and a couple of dates that never made me fly or climax. I never mentioned Robert's name. I am sure I did not."

"But Evelyn, everyone knew I was your friend, and they knew I had been dating Robert. Maybe one of the gang members is impersonating Robert and had the birthmark created by a tattoo?"

"Connie, you are being paranoid, and I understand why given what you have been through. It is difficult to accept that Robert has come back into your life, but it is very unrealistic to believe that it isn't him."

As she poured her third glass of wine, Connie was comforted by Evelyn's thoughts even though Evelyn did not have a history of excellent judgment. Connie had witnessed her making many poor decisions in the past two decades. Men she chose to date were the most glaring. However, parental decisions were a close second. Connie couldn't love her any more deeply as her best friend even though she recognized her shortcomings. Connie thought that Evelyn probably felt the same way about her although they had never discussed it.

Connie walked the one mile on Harlem streets, and by the time she arrived at her two-bedroom apartment, she was mentally exhausted. She needed to sleep and stop thinking. When her head reached the pillow, she was not only thinking of where Robert, Jr. might be, but also, what the alleged Robert, Sr. might be doing. Was the real Robert nervously awaiting her decision to have dinner with him, or was the fictitious Robert hanging out at a poolroom with Robert, Jr.

5

Freedom Flight

The emotion Jeffrey sensed as he walked by the tarnished steel rods that endlessly intersected from concrete ceiling to concrete floor was most definitely overwhelming. He didn't focus on the feeling even though it was most penetrating, as his mind was mired in anticipation of who was waiting for him at the end of this liberating walk. He hadn't seen a woman in six years, and the thought of being alone with, or touching a woman, was all his mind could manage. When he first walked this hallway, in the opposite direction, he had lost hope of ever feeling the warmth of femininity again. Although he had never been successful in a relationship for any duration, his desire for female connection continued to be ever present.

As the guard preceded him around the last corner, he could see a woman he didn't recognize standing alone. She didn't look at all like the pictures he had been receiving. Her short brown hair had replaced that of the long flowing blond beauty. This woman's very slender frame was unlike the voluptuous body he had been salivating about on a daily basis. Her face was tired, almost worn beyond comprehension. She looked seventy-five, not fifty-five. Could this possibly be the woman who had been writing very personal letters to him every week? In those letters, she had revealed details of her anxieties, hopes, and disappointments that he would only expect to read in a personal diary. It had amazed him that she would expose herself in this manner to a perfect stranger. He constrained his impulse to ask her bluntly if she was the woman in those pictures. It would be offensive and serve no immediate purpose, he surmised. She had made this trip to take him to freedom: that was enough for now.

"Are you Jenny?"

"Yes, I am."

She knew he must be disappointed by her appearance. She also thought he didn't look any different. He had apparently physically weathered his confinement without experiencing a decline in health. She was certain from his letters that the mental strain had been devastating. She was eager to do everything she could to erase that memory.

"Where would you like our first stop to be? A restaurant, a bar, or perhaps, a bathtub? What have you missed the most?"

Jeffrey knew what he missed the most but wasn't about to tell this plain looking woman. He felt no lust, no chemistry, not even an emotional interest as he assessed her lack of femininity. Given the erections her letters and pictures had generated, it was a disappointment for sure,

"A walk in the park, I want to feel the grass under my feet and look at the sky forever."

Her smile conveyed sincerity as she led him out the door after he gathered his personal items from the discharge clerk. That smile did remind him of her endearing letters.

She wanted to hold his hand as they walked across the parking lot; however, she knew that would make him uncomfortable. She wasn't what he was expecting and could only hope that at some point in time, he would share her desire for emotional and physical intimacy. She had been waiting for a very long time and considered her patience a virtue. If he wanted sex, given his long absence of satisfaction and even without intimate feelings for her, she would oblige. Although realizing it might never happen, she was determined to claw her way into his emotions. His letters left no doubt that he craved sexual release with a woman. She would provide the best she knew how to fulfill his craving. She had read books and even purchased sex videos to enhance his first experience after the prolonged drought. In his letters, he had revealed very distasteful sexual advances from other inmates. She realized those experiences might generate a psychological problem for him. She had even taken a night school course to better understand how to deal with that possible impediment. The instructor had provided very helpful personal insight, and she was confident that she could help him if that mental barrier existed. He had surprised her by including the experiences in his letters, and she now understood he needed to tell someone. Keeping it a secret would only magnify his inhibitions.

She had learned not to ask him about the details but was prepared to reply when he was ready to unfold his feelings. She thought if he opened up to her about intimate experiences, it might generate a positive emotional connection between them. At that point, if it ever happened, hopefully the pictures she sent him would become a vague memory. The course study had convinced her that emotional intimacy and openness to discuss anything created an even stronger bond than great sex. Both together were the ultimate relationship.

He walked slowly outside the gate and felt like he could have walked forever. Never again would he take freedom for granted.

"How far is the park?"

"About two hours. Put the window down if you want some fresh air."

Without hesitation, he gulped the breeze. It was a sunny June day, and it felt like he was being transported by a spiritual power. He had never been a religious person, and his wrongful conviction hadn't generated a closer relationship with the Creator. He always considered himself a good person but living with the locked-up felons had definitely changed his outlook. Being a good person had not brought him any peace, only misery. The rapists and child molesters that had been his social life for six years had soured his goodness. Fate was subjecting him to the same punishment as the scum of society. Fortunately, he had been spared any family to witness his demise. As a bank Vice- President, he felt a sense of accomplishment but that evaporated when he heard the jury foreman pronounce 'GUILTY'. He wished he had embezzled the half-million dollars that the twelve individuals had concluded was his sin. If he had, he could now sail away to a peaceful, solitary life. As it was, the sentencing fine had left him destitute. He knew he was smart enough to steal without being caught, and also knew what financial treasure was vulnerable. His universe was now indebted to him, and he had planned for six years how to get even. This plain woman, whoever she really was, had become an integral part of his plan. She obviously was vulnerable, or she wouldn't have had an emotional attachment to a "felon-stranger". The universe was going to serve her a sentence, also. He knew how to pretend to be a good guy. All he had to do was act like his old self. The imprisoned Jeffrey, he concluded, was his mind-set now. His new mental agenda was to take advantage of anyone to preserve your own welfare. The universe had not shielded him from being framed, and he didn't intend to respect any part of society. The thought of getting even had enabled him to endure the scum existence, and he was eager to fulfill his newfound dream. It was time to get the plan started with the stranger behind the wheel.

"Two hours may be too long before we eat, and we have a lot to talk about. I want to look in your eyes while we talk. Let's stop and get to know each other visually while we are still dressed."

His overt intention for sex came as a surprise to Jenny. She expected the inquiring questions about the pictures and her appearance. She was glad sex was apparently going to come first. His long drought apparently was overpowering his disappointment about the intentionally misleading pictures. That was just fine with her. She was prepared to satisfy him all day if that was his desire. His complete satisfaction was her only hope of capturing his long-term interest. A place to live, good cooking, and her constant affection were her plan. She had made this offer in her letters. His responses welcomed the proposal.

"Does this restaurant look OK?"

"Sure, anyone works for me. I am not sure I remember how to order from a menu, but I know I want pancakes and ham. You may need to remind me to eat slowly as I haven't done that in a very long time. It was intimidating to know the man sitting beside you would steal your food if he had the opportunity. I, also, would steal his. It was survival of the fittest. If you didn't act tough, you were doomed to constant oppression. I had a steep learning curve in prison. Being a banker most of my life made me educated in life skills but not survival skills. It was either learn to be tough or wither like a bird with no feathers. My Marine Corps experiences as a young man were my best asset. My native intelligence was of less value."

As they slid into the booth, she noticed him looking at her legs. She had purposefully worn a short skirt. Her legs and chest were her best assets, she thought. She also had dressed to expose some cleavage. That wasn't her normal behavior. However, she had planned every detail to entice his interest in taking her to bed. She had told him in her letters that she had very little experience with sex and hoped he didn't mind teaching her. She had read that it was a turn-on for men to teach a woman to be good at providing sexual satisfaction. In his responsive letters, that information rang true. He had even asked her if she was skilled in oral sex, and if she enjoyed it. She responded honestly that she had never engaged in that manner of sex and looked forward to learning what he could teach her. She hoped that while sitting alone in his cell and reading her willingness to learn how to use her tongue would enlarge his penis while thinking of her. That thought aroused her, as well. She had been anticipating his sexual desire for her for nearly thirty years. Her interest began shortly after she went to work for the bank as a teller who had just graduated from community college.

"Can I get you something to drink?"

"I will have coffee with cream," he blurted out.

Jenny had expected better manners. Apparently, prison had erased the memory of that attribute. She hoped living a caring life would restore his former self. She had only observed his behavior sporadically when he visited her branch for meetings with the manager. He had always been courteous; however, he didn't engage in personal conversations with the branch employees. Despite his professional aloofness, she was smitten by his appearance and display of character. Every time she witnessed his presence, she could feel his strong arms lifting her above his head to caress her hard nipples with his tongue. That image had sustained her desire for all these years. No other man had penetrated that desire. No other man had touched her breasts in fantasy or the real world that she endured. She had been raped at age sixteen just before she entered community college. The two boys had only removed her shorts and panties to take their pleasure. Her breasts remained virgin. Someday she hoped to tell Jeffrey that her nipples were his private domain. She fantasized about his tongue devouring her large breasts and anything else he might want to explore. This daydream prevailed to the exclusion of even thinking about him penetrating her. The two boys who had violated her left her without any longing to feel that sensation again. She expected that probably would be an initial priority for Jeffrey. No doubt she would have to wait for the fulfillment she fantasized. When she had satisfied him, his focus could be directed to her nipples while she enlarged his penis again with her fingers. She had even practiced the techniques she read about with inanimate objects. She hoped she had mastered the skills necessary to be successful. While practicing, she did wonder what his penis would feel like in her hand. Would it generate her pleasure or be only an exercise as the practice had been?

"Bring me pancakes and ham."

"We don't serve pancakes after 11 A.M., sir. We do have eggs."

"Well, you should have pancakes!"

Jenny was embarrassed by his rudeness. This wasn't the memory she had of Jeffrey.

"Do you have French toast?"

"Not after 11."

"Give me three eggs over easy. No brown on the outside edge."

"I will tell the cook how you like them."

Jenny thought the waitress was very polite despite his manner.

"What will you have, Miss?"

"Do you poach eggs?"

"Yes, we do."

"Make mine poached then", he abruptly interrupted.

Jenny was amazed that the waitress maintained her pleasant demeanor despite Jeffrey's rudeness. She concluded that her plan may be in jeopardy. "TLC" might not be enough to rehab this hardened and mean-spirited "stranger."

"I will have two poached and bacon, thank you."

After depositing Jeffrey's coffee and cream, the waitress disappeared to the kitchen and breathed a sigh of relief.

"I don't know how that woman tolerates that man. She doesn't wear a wedding ring and that is a good thing. What does she see in him? No man is that good in bed even if he has nine inches."

"It must be money; that is the only thing that tops sex", the other waitress replied.

"I would rather be a poor waitress than put-up with that SOB."

The polite waitress had dropped her "act" of professionalism and exposed her real self.

"If it were me, I would steal his money while he was in 'after-glow'. I would disappear and then haunt him with mailed notes telling him how much I was enjoying the Caribbean", the other waitress responded.

After serving the poached eggs, the waitress was relieved to provide service to a different table. It would require some time for her to normalize her attitude. She couldn't rationalize a very few customers, like this belligerent man, who were overtly nasty.

6

The shop door was difficult to open pushing against the three inches of snow that had fallen overnight. Connie had decided not to tell Alice the truth about the stranger's visit yesterday. She wasn't sure what the truth was and didn't want to explain all that. It bothered her considerably to be dishonest; however, she couldn't manage to explain what remained confusing.

"Good morning, Connie," she heard Alice's greeting. "I will shovel the snow on the sidewalk before I take off my coat and scarf."

"Alice, before we get busy with customers," and they both chuckled, "I owe you an explanation about the man who visited me yesterday. He was a close personal friend of Robert, Jr.'s father and received a letter from Robert in China, and he sent me some money. I haven't seen him since Robert left."

"Then Robert is still alive?"

"Apparently so," Connie answered with an inflection of resentment." The letter was mailed from Beijing with no return address".

"Did you read the letter? Did he say anything about you?"

"I read it, and no, only to give me some money."

Alice wanted to ask how much money but knew it wasn't her place to do so. If Connie wanted her to know she would tell her.

"Well, at least you know that he has developed a conscience and some sense of responsibility. I wonder what might have happened in his life to cause that."

"It appears that I will never get the answer to that or a thousand other questions I have."

"Are you going to see Robert's friend again?"

"I don't have any plans to."

Connie felt a little better having finished her false story. She even partly wished that the story was true, and then she wouldn't have to reconcile her feelings about Robert Young. She was still very conflicted about him and continued to be uncomfortable with his story.

She once had been deeply in love with Robert Young, and now only felt indifference even when she considered his story to be true. In her daydreams of Robert returning, she ran to his arms and kissed him endlessly and hard. She hadn't experienced those dreams for many years: ever since convincing herself that he was dead.

Alice had gone out to shovel the sidewalk while Connie silently dealt with her emotions. It was Friday and Evelyn usually came to her place if she didn't have a date. A date was scheduled tonight so Connie would go home and fix a little dinner and read a novel. Reading immersed her in other people's lives and reduced her stress. She would have gone to movies but couldn't afford that, or cable TV channels. Watching the morning and evening news while eating was the extent of her interest. The constant bickering and endless gridlock among lawmakers in Washington, D.C. was annoying and upsetting. Voting had never been important to her, and the TV news only confirmed her disinterest. Having the financial bonanza, she now enjoyed would enable her to seek new avenues of entertainment. The theater musicals and plays might even be possible. Evelyn didn't have any interest in that venue, but perhaps Alice would like to accompany her. She had become so accustomed to retreating in her small two-bedroom apartment that the thought of "going out" had made her uncomfortable. Surprisingly, she even felt excited about embarking on a new life. Except for Robert, Jr., her mind had relaxed, and she felt less stress.

When Alice came in from the cold, Connie asked her to sit and have coffee with her.

"Alice, if I move the shop uptown, would you be willing to ride the subway if I paid your fare?"

Alice was startled by the question and stammered as she said: "Why would you move?"

"I have been approached by one of our customers offering to be a partner if I move to a higher income location. She has a dry-cleaning business in the neighborhood and can provide very nice used clothing for us to merchandise. Some of her customers only wear their clothes once or twice before leaving them to be cleaned and never pick them up. Apparently, in their social circles, they can't be seen twice in the same outfit. After cleaning, she is willing to give us the clothes to sell and split the profits. In return, she will offer a 50% discount to the donating customers. Their husbands have their suits and ties cleaned and pressed frequently. They need to make space in their closets for new clothes and that is why they leave the old ones. The new location will mean all new customers, and we both will miss our current customers. Maybe a few of them will travel the subway to come and see us but most will not be interested in those clothes. I possibly could make a lot more money, and if I do, I will raise your pay."

It was a lot for Alice to digest, nevertheless she said: "Of course, I will travel if that is what you want to do. Do I know the customer that is going to be your partner?"

"I don't think you have met her. She has only been in the shop a couple of times. She made her offer a few weeks ago and, perhaps, she is no longer interested. I am uneasy with the risk of a new location and acquiring new customers, but it would be nice for both of us to be more successful. I am going to call her and see if the proposal still stands. If it does, I would like for us to visit the location on Sunday to check it out. Is your schedule open on Sunday?"

"Sure, I can go. I would like to offer my opinion on its suitability. Could we also visit the dry-cleaning shop and see some of the clothes?"

"That is a good idea, I hadn't thought of that."

7

Connie punched the keypad with the numbers she had been given and heard: "Mei Lin's Dry Cleaning."

"May I speak to Mei Lin?"

"I will get her."

She heard another number being selected and then a ring.

"Hello. This is Mei Lin," uttered the broken English she had heard in the shop a few weeks ago.

"This is Connie Taylor from the 92nd Street consignment shop."

"Yes, good to hear you. You want to open new store?"

"I would like to come Sunday morning and see the space and your dry-cleaning place."

"You come 11 A.M. to address on card, Good-bye".

Connie wasn't put-off by the cold reception as she understood the culture. Many of her customers were similarly oriented.

When she arrived home that February night, most of her anxiety had dissipated. She was surprised by her overture to relocate her store. After reflection, she credited it to the "Robert-Stranger" arrival and feeling rich.

She and her much older sister had grown up in a poor neighborhood with an alcoholic father. She had never even imagined having enough money to spoil herself. She was elated that Alice was supportive of the potential move. Her maturity at age 28 was a valuable asset to the business. Alice had been working with her for nearly all of the eight years that she had the shop. She was very personable, and the customers seemed to prefer her to herself. Connie recognized that she wasn't "bubbly" like Alice, and her disability was obviously unattractive. She had the stroke just a year after opening the shop and suspected that the stress of that decision, added to her daily living stress, was the culprit. Alice, when just a new employee, had to totally manage the new business for six months during her recovery. She would not have the shop were it not for Alice who had previous retail experience, but her job evaporated when the store owner closed due to illness. The previous business merchandised new clothes, and the used clothes sales position initially felt demeaning. Years later, she told Connie that managing the store in her absence had changed her disappointment. Engaging with lower income patrons had become more satisfying than demeaning. Connie wondered if dealing with upper-income class customers would be as rewarding for both of them.

Shortly after she finished eating a ham slice and green beans, a knock on the door alarmed her. I certainly hope that isn't Robert, she thought. I am not ready to talk to him. When she opened the door, she was surprised to see Evelyn.

"I cancelled my date thought we should talk. Did Robert come to the shop?"

"No, but I thought I saw him standing across the street. Maybe he wanted me to see him and call him over. I don't know."

"Have you decided when you're going to see him?"

"No, I'm not ready. I am going Sunday to look at a new location for the store."

"Why do you want to move?"

Connie revealed Mei Lin's proposal and Evelyn inquired: "Wouldn't you lose all of your customers?"

"Probably, and that is scary, but I could possibly make a lot more money."

"You don't need money now."

"I would like to be more successful and pay Alice better. She struggles, and I know all too well the toll that takes. Would you like to come with us Sunday morning?"

"No, I rescheduled my date for tomorrow night, and I might be in bed late Sunday morning. I went out with George last weekend, and I'm looking forward to the encore. We stopped short of going to bed, but I don't expect that to happen tomorrow night. He was a gentleman and I appreciate that. He is a really good kisser and has strong legs. He rides a bicycle all the time: to work and everywhere. He works in construction and seems to have enough money to take us out to dinner every weekend. He isn't really handsome, but I guess I can't expect everything. He is a candidate for the long-term. When are you going to date again? It has been two years, hasn't it?"

"I just don't have any interest in meeting a man. All those back and forth questions about who you are: all the game-playing and kissing a man who doesn't know how to kiss while he is feeling your ass. I would rather read a good novel about a woman having a satisfying relationship and great sex."

"Well, I don't see how reading about it can substitute for the real thing. I never had an orgasm while reading a book!"

"Orgasms are not that great unless I am flying and that only happened with Robert. Don't expect it to happen again."

"Connie, <u>THAT</u> is your answer! Have sex with the man who gave you that check and see what happens when you stroke the bird on the back of his neck. If you soar like you remember, it will prove it is Robert."

Connie chuckled at the thought and replied: "I have zero interest in sleeping with that man, whoever he is. I don't feel any chemistry with him."

"Maybe that will change after you get more answers. Maybe the chemistry will reappear if it really is Robert. Maybe your fear is preventing the chemistry?"

"Evelyn, I have an idea: why don't <u>YOU</u> have sex with him and see if you lift off the ground."

"Connie, if Robert is as good as you remember, I would gladly have sex with him. Just for you, of course." They both laughed.

"Be my surrogate, Evelyn, with my blessing. Obviously, if he is Robert, I don't desire him any longer. In fact, if you dated him, you could learn a lot more about the truth or fiction. As I think about it, I would really like you to get the answers: to see if he tells you the same story, he is telling me."

"I can do that. This is getting exciting, like playing detective. How do I meet him? Do you want to introduce us?"

"Let's think through this, Evelyn. He said he has been following me for two months. If so, he may have seen us together. We need to find out if he has seen you. If he really is Robert, and I doubt it, he might not want to jump in bed with you right away."

"He could still have feelings for you, Connie, and not be interested in me."

"Evelyn, every man you meet wants to get his hands all over you, and if this stranger doesn't, it will tell us something. However, if we find out that he knows we are friends, it will affect his interest. Not friends, and NOT Robert---he will pursue you like every other horny man. Friends, and NOT Robert---but pretending to be, he will be reluctant to 'move on you' unless I promote the idea. Friends, and REALLY Robert, he would ask my permission before he dated you. That is the Robert I remember. If he no longer has any feelings for me, although he told me that he loved me 22 years ago, he will still want my OK to date you. He would need to know that he is not hurting me. Not friends, and REALLY Robert, if he wants to take you to bed, we will know for sure that he is here to help Robert, Jr., and not to be romantically involved with me."

"Whoa Connie! That was way too confusing for me. You play detective, and I will play seducer. If you start to have feelings for your stranger, tell me and I will immediately back off. However, if I have already soared, that won't be easy. I am already anxious to meet your visitor and have lost some interest in George. Hopefully, George will re-motivate me with his next kiss. I expect he will. We still haven't decided how I'm going to meet the 'would-be' Robert."

"Evelyn, I think you should just meet him when he is hanging out someplace and see if he recognizes you. I need to find out where he goes to eat or drink so I will need to meet him. If I see him tomorrow, I will talk to him."

By now, the wine bottle was near empty and both women had a buzz. Their conversation had been so stimulating, they were not aware they had been drinking heavily. As they were discussing the possibility of opening another bottle of Yellow Tail, another much stronger knock was heard. It was nearly 11 P.M, and the unexpected sound was alarming for both women.

"Who is it?" Connie asked.

"Mom, it is me. Is it OK to come in? I thought you might have a visitor when I saw the light on."

"Yes, Robert. It is only Evelyn. How good to see you! Are you going to spend the night?"

"No. I only came to get some clothes and leave the dirty ones. Hello, Evelyn."

"Hi, Robert, you get better looking all the time. If I were 25, I would have you lassoed."

"I see so little of you. Are you staying at a girlfriend's house?"

He smiled and said: "I should be so lucky. My 'buds' and I just decided to go tubing in the Adirondacks. We are leaving now and will be on the slopes in the morning."

"Can't you sit awhile and talk with us?"

"I wish I could, but the guys are waiting on me."

He went to his bedroom, which he rarely slept in, and commenced opening drawers. Connie felt blessed that he was always respectful. His bitterness towards life did not include her.

"When will you be back from sledding?"

"Who knows? When we get bored, I guess."

"Will you call me to let me know you're alright?"

"Sure, mom. See you soon: Bye, Evelyn." He left as quickly as he entered.

"That boy's life is a complete mystery to me. He has never brought one of his friends' home since he dropped out of High School in his junior year. He finished that truck-driving school when he was 17. I don't know how he got away with lying about his age. I also don't know how he gets his money and that is what really worries me. When I ask, he just replies: 'I get by'. At least he doesn't lie to me about it but it must not be legal or he would tell me."

"Connie, I know it worries you something awful, but you are powerless to help which is why you should let your 'Robert-stranger" find out what he's doing."

"You're probably right but if he causes Robert, Jr. to be arrested, I will never forgive myself. I want you to meet him and get some answers before I tell him to approach Robert, Jr. Maybe he already knows Robert, Jr. I can't be sure about that. I've got to find out about that damn bird on his neck. If he is an imposter, find out for me. If he isn't, I will let him help his son."

8

Freedom Flight

Jenny broke the uneasy silence: "Do you still plan to invest your time determining who framed your embezzlement?"

"First, I need to find employment. As a convicted felon, working in the financial industry isn't going to be possible. It is the only business I know. Perhaps I will become a bank robber. That is an occupation that fits my education. Banks have vulnerabilities that I could exploit."

"Wouldn't you be concerned that if you were caught, you would go back to prison, which made you feel trapped every day?"

"I wouldn't go back to prison. I would kill myself before I was arrested. I have had a lot of time to devise my plan. Would you like to be my accomplice?"

The question shocked Jenny, and she was unable to answer. Her racing thoughts only created confusion in her mind. Her silence was now mind numbing. Perhaps her devotion for this man's attention had been a total mistake for all these years. Perhaps he wasn't the pillar of strength she had always expected him to be. Her concerns about the character of the man she was looking at across the table were escalating significantly in just the past thirty minutes. Perhaps she didn't want him in her bed, or even in her house. Was it too late to retreat?

"I can see my question upset you. I said it in jest although I would accept any help you decide to give me. I probably will not rob a bank. It is just my anger at being framed that generates such thoughts."

She was relieved to hear the man she had adored from afar for most of her life was not going to destroy her imagery. Her consoling thought was her plan to restore his goodness or die trying. She had managed to care for a distraught loved one in the past when her sister had recovered from a stroke, and it made her feel a great deal of satisfaction. During her rehab, Connie had been mad at the world for the life that fate had generated. Being twelve years older, Jenny was more like a mother than a sister. The age difference had prevented any close sibling bonding. Their mother died when Jenny was eighteen and Connie only six. Jenny later realized that she had not devoted any quality time with her childhood sister that she deserved and needed. She was too pre-occupied with her own personal interests at that time, and still recovering emotionally from her rape. She felt guilty that Connie was emotionally deprived of affection all of her childhood. Their father was a mean alcoholic and did little more than provide food and shelter. When Connie suffered her stroke, she traveled to New York from Chicago to help in any way she could. The bank had approved her request for leave of absence, and she remained with Connie for two months. During that period, they confided in each other, discussing their perils and hopes for the future as well as their childhood challenges. Connie didn't remember much about her mother as she had been sick for two years before her death. Jenny filled in the missing details. Although they bonded closely during those two months, their communication lapsed when Jenny returned to Chicago. They mailed Christmas cards with short notes. Jenny had observed during her visit that Robert, Jr. was not on a good path. He was rebellious and angry. She did wonder how his life had developed. Connie never wrote about him nor did she ever discuss his father during her stay in New York.

"How are your eggs and ham?"

"Just fine, I apologize for my shortness with the waitress. It isn't her fault they don't serve pancakes after 11. It will take me awhile to not over-react to disappointment. Being on the offensive has been my defense during my confinement."

Jenny wanted to counsel him to apologize to the waitress but thought better of it. His recognition of his negative attitude was enough for now; a good sign that the goodness was buried but could be excavated.

"Are you ready to drive to the park?"

"Let's leave the park for later. I would rather go directly to your house."

9

Sunday morning Connie met Alice at the subway, and they exited at Stop #3 on the Uptown Line. Neither one of them had ever visited that neighborhood. To say it was upscale was an understatement: row after row of beautiful exteriors. They could only imagine what the inside of those apartments looked like. Both Connie and Alice were uncomfortable: immensely uncomfortable! They looked at each other with the same expression---how could we relate to the people who live here? They walked to Mei Lin's business. It was not what they expected. It was in a very large, newly renovated building. The signage was a subdued flashing blue and green- "DRY CLEANING" in the window. No mention of Mei Lin's name. The front door looked similar to all the neighborhood apartment doors. It must have been eight feet high and outlined in dark mahogany. If not for the flashing sign, it provided no evidence of a dry-cleaning establishment. The apartment sized windows had attractive curtains providing no view of dry cleaning. Mei Lin was standing inside the door when they arrived and greeted them.

"You come, good."

"This is Alice, my friend and helper."

"I see you in store. Very nice with people. Look at clothes for you to sell."

Only then did Connie notice a professionally prepared small sign printed on both sides, through the window curtains: "Trade Clothes For 50% Off Men's Cleaning". Connie thought: she has already concluded that I will accept her offer. The women's' clothes to be sold looked brand new and very stylish. They showed no sign of wear and could easily be valued at 50% of the original retail price. If the clientele were available, a $300 ensemble would be saleable for $150 without much effort.: $75 profit on a sale. Many days her total sales were less than $75. It struck her that she was already thinking upscale Manhattan rather than Harlem.

Alice announced: "These clothes would fly off the racks if they are properly displayed."

"Your shop through door": and Mei Lin opened the door to what appeared to be a large vacant bedroom. In fact, it actually was two large bedrooms. The front bedroom had a balcony door leading to the street corner with a separate outside entrance from the dry-cleaning shop.

Alice instantly proclaimed: "We could serve tea on that balcony!"

"People walk into cleaning shop and walk out your balcony. No one knows clothes not new but buyer."

"Mei Lin, I could never afford to rent this space. It is too expensive."

"No rent, my building. Two apartments upstairs for living."

Connie and Alice looked at each other in disbelief. Both thought: no need for subway or going outside on cold mornings.

"Mei Lin, this is too much. Why are you doing this?"

"Building empty. Need someone. My 50% good money, no bother renters. I send truck get your clothes racks and furniture".

"Mei Lin, this is a very generous offer, but it would be a very big change in our lives. Alice and I need to talk about this."

"You sit. Talk. I bring coffee", and she exited to her cleaning establishment.

"Connie, just so you know, I would love to live in the upstairs apartment. If you don't want to do this, I will do it on my own."

Connie thought: certainly, that is possible. Alice didn't need her, except for the business license. Alice was an illegal immigrant existing on a "DACA" exemption so she would not qualify for a business license. She could own the shop and Alice could manage it. When Mei Lin returned with two cups in hand, Connie offered Alice's interest. With no hesitation, Mei Lin responded in a negative manner.

"Connie must run shop or offer no work."

"Why?" Connie responded.

"Need American woman to meet customers. No foreigners like me. People buy used clothes from American owner only, not foreigners."

That was a revelation to Connie but certainly insightful. These rich women were, no doubt, class snobby. Despite her reservation, she did not want to disappoint Alice, who was excited about moving. Last night, her mind was resisting change, and now she was considering a very different life.

10

Robert, Jr., after departing the subway, climbed in the SUV and the five young men drove into the night. They were steering for the Adirondacks. After ten minutes, they arrived at a warehouse entrance identified as "MANHATTAN DISCOUNT FURNITURE." Robert, Jr. went inside and got behind the wheel of the tractor trailer. Another member of the gang started the engine of a small PENSKE truck. The three vehicles convoyed up the highway. They arrived at a truck stop and rented sleeping rooms. The plan had been detailed-designed by the unknown "master-mind" and would be executed in the morning.

The destination address was a three-million-dollar estate adjacent to a dozen other similar properties. A Century 21 sign was prominently visible in the front yard. Two vehicles entered the driveway: a Penske truck and an SUV with Century 21 signage. One of the four young men cut the alarm wires while another used bolt cutter to open the locked key box. One thief stood inside the window watching, and Robert. Jr. was standing guard on the street. Any suspicious vehicles arriving would be signaled by Robert. Jr. The other three quickly went to the intended objects: Artwork, jewelry and silverware as well as other valuables. The items were placed in plain cardboard boxes, and within thirty minutes, the five men had vanished into the maze of traffic. They drove five minutes to an abandoned building parking lot and drove the Penske truck into the Manhattan Discount Furniture semi-trailer. Quickly they stacked the boxes behind the Penske truck to hide its existence. The Century 21 magnetic door strip was removed from the SUV, and the two vehicles drove off separately. Robert. Jr. and a companion headed south to the warehouse. They unloaded the boxes and the Penske truck was parked alongside a U-Haul and Budget truck. They had another job planned in a few days and would use the Budget vehicle. The "Master-Mind" had scoped out another residence in Hartford, Connecticut. Meanwhile, he would "fence-off" the stolen goods to one of three established outlets. This plan had been providing all of them with prosperity for three years. Using false identification, the "Master-Mind" posed as a prospective buyer and inventoried the items to be "boxed-up" during his visit. His next target would always be at least 150 miles distant and listed with a different real estate firm. He waited at least six months after his house inspection before scheduling the "take'. That timing lowered his risk of being suspected. Fake driver licenses with matching fake car plates and utilizing different cars on a daily basis camouflaged his identity. None of Robert, Jr.'s gang knew his identity. As directed by courier notes delivered to the pool hall, Robert, Jr. trucked the cardboard boxes to different warehouses. He had been recruited at the pool hall by Pete after revealing that he had a CDL license. His passion was shooting pool, and he had a natural talent. He was virtually unbeatable locally. No longer would the locals play him money games. Occasionally, an out-of-towner would show up to challenge his reputation. He didn't meet any young women while chasing his passion, and rarely missed the experience. Women didn't seem to be necessary in his life. However, his "buds" were always talking about their conquests with never any mention of love.

He had purchased a small travel trailer and usually slept in the campground. Given his "line of work", he didn't want to get his mother exposed in the event he was identified as a thief and followed. He wanted to help her financially, but she wouldn't accept his money. She had told him very little about this father except that he was a government security guard. He found it ironic for a burglar to be the son of a security guard.

11

James observed Connie's movements from afar for two days after visiting the shop and accompanying her to deposit the check. Her activities, except for the Sunday morning visit to the dry-cleaning shop, had not changed with her new-found wealth. He wasn't surprised as he did not assess her as impulsive. She was the opposite: cautious and slow to make decisions.

Although he hadn't told Connie, he had met Robert Jr. two months earlier in the pool hall. In fact, he had shot pool with him several times, always losing in close contests. He observed a young man who was masking a pleasant personality with anger. He wasn't close to his "buds" and didn't share his life with them, except for playing pool. They respected him but didn't bond with him. They didn't know where he lived or anything about him personally except that he was a truck driver. When they asked a personal question, he was evasive. They had accepted his secretive nature and knew they could count on him to do his job. They discussed their thoughts on his private life among themselves. Some of them suspected he was gay and kept the closet door tightly locked. They had invited him to go to the bar with them to "hit-on" girls; however, he always declined saying: "I would rather shoot pool". James knew this as he had engaged with Robert, Jr.'s "buds" a couple of times at the bar. James had told them he had recently moved to Manhattan as he needed to get out of Chicago but provided no further explanation. They wondered if he had fled the law but never asked him. They saw him as a possible addition to their team if ever needed. They told the pool hall owner and recruiter, Pete, about him and he responded: "I will check him out. He could be undercover law." James knew all of this as one of the gang members had a loose tongue. If Pete knew about the loose tongue, there would be hell to pay. James thought he might be able to use that information to his advantage at some point. If Connie agreed to let him help with Robert, Jr., he had a plan in mind.

12

Connie was anxious to tell Evelyn about her moving decision and called her as soon as she arrived home on Sunday.

"Will you travel uptown to visit me if I move? Can we still have our in-depth talks over wine?"

"Why would you move? I thought you were going to ride the subway."

Connie told her what had transpired during the visit.

"Connie, it is unbelievable what is happening to you. Did you find religion or what?"

"I can't believe it, either Evelyn. It is like I am no longer me. I am not comfortable with the new me and hope that will change. In some ways, the stress was better than the discomfort I feel now."

"Connie, do you still want me to meet your "Robert-stranger?".

"Yes, I am ready to talk to him when, or if, he shows up again. I want to know what he thinks he can do for Robert, Jr. He says his name now is James Whitmore so we should probably start to call him James. How did your date with George turn out?"

"He left after breakfast this morning and was all smiles. He is a good lover, and I hope he sticks around awhile."

Connie spent Sunday evening thinking about her shop move and her personal move. The one-bedroom apartment would not have any space for Robert Jr. She wanted him to have a place and decided she could keep her old apartment for him as her new apartment would be rent-free. If things didn't work out with the new store, she would have the old apartment to return to. That thought eased much of her discomfort. Mei Lin had said she would send a truck: She should start packing. They would need to pack the store fixtures, also. The consigned clothes needed to be returned to their owners. She would ask Alice to call current customers tomorrow and ask them to pick up their goods. Her building lease had expired years ago, and she could leave at her pleasure. Her expenses would also be reduced as she wouldn't have to pay rent any longer. All in all, she felt pretty good about the changes. She would leave Robert, Jr. a note if he didn't come home before she moved. He had his own key and now his own apartment. It must have been extrasensory as just then the phone rang, and it was James Whitmore.

"Connie, can I please have lunch or dinner with you? Robert, Jr. left town Friday night with his gang. I am really concerned about his activities. He could go to jail, and we don't want that."

"I will meet you for dinner tomorrow night. Where do you usually eat?"

"I will meet you wherever you want to go, Connie."

"Let's go where I can have a glass of wine. I will probably need it. I never go out and drink, so you pick a place where you drink".

"OK, let's meet at Georgio's on 2nd Street at 6:30."

Connie immediately called Evelyn.

"Can you walk into Georgio's on 2nd Street about 7 tomorrow night? I am having dinner with James Whitmore. Just sit at the bar where you can be easily seen but don't let on that you know me."

"Absolute, I know Georgio's well: I have eaten there several times with dates. It seems to be a popular place for "hook-ups" …always plenty of single men and women there. I wonder if that is why James knows the place. How are you going to have us meet?"

"I am not. I just want you to see each other. If he has seen you visit my apartment, he might mention it; although, he could recognize it as a set-up and say nothing. Either way, his reaction or non-reaction might reveal something. I will leave the restaurant alone and maybe you will have the chance to talk with him. Don't move too fast like your normal self. Act somewhat aloof and disinterested: Don't give him your phone number, but if he asks, agree to meet him again."

"Why not seduce him and get some answers right now?"

"Too risky. Let it develop slowly."

"Connie, if I see that bird it will not be easy to go slow."

"Well, make a date with George to quell your urge! Just kidding. See you tomorrow, but only see you. Good night."

Monday was a busy day with packing at the store and Alice returning clothes. Connie hung a window sign announcing the closing of the shop on Saturday. Sunday, she had scheduled the truck with

Mei Lin. Wednesday evening, she and Alice planned to visit their new apartments again for a more detailed look at possible furniture arrangements. The flurry of activity limited the time her mind focused on tonight's dinner with James.

13

Freedom Flight

During the second hour's drive home to Lincoln Park, Jeffrey asked most of the questions. Jenny was glad he was talking politely.

"In your letter you told me that you moved to Chicago from New York some thirty years ago. What brought you here?"

"After College, I needed to leave New York. Too many bad memories. I liked the big city environment and Chicago seemed like a good choice. I could mingle with different people every day and occasionally meet someone to have coffee or lunch with. I enjoy learning about other people's lives. Mine has been very boring."

"Did it take you long to find a job at the bank?"

"No, I saw an ad in the paper and was hired immediately to train as a teller. It gave me the opportunity to meet many new people. A few of them became friends but I never made a close friend."

"You have been without a close friend all these years?"

"Pretty much."

"Did you date many men? You said you have never been married."

Jenny wasn't ready to tell him about her rape and didn't expect to ever be comfortable discussing it with anyone.

"Very few. They apparently didn't find me very interesting."

She had to lie as he would know in short order that she wasn't a virgin. She had been asked out a few times by bank customers but turned them down for fear of a sexual advance. Each time she felt disillusioned that she couldn't enjoy a man's interest. She knew they would eventually, if not sooner, expect more than conversation.

"Did you find them interesting?"

"Yes, sometimes."

"Why did you find me interesting?"

"I read about your arrest on the front page of the newspaper. When I listened to you during your TV interview, it didn't seem to me that you were guilty. Your words were very convincing, and I am a believer in body language. Working in a bank myself and seeing the real possibilities of a fraud being committed, I felt how terrible it would be to go to jail for something you didn't do. I decided to support you if you would permit me."

"Do you have any family?"

Jeffrey didn't really care about her personal situation; however, he knew he needed to act like he did if he was going to convince her to help him with his plan. Even though she was retired, she knew bank procedures and could be a valuable resource. She was obviously needy for a man's attention, and he could take easy advantage of that vulnerability.

"Only one sister who still lives in Manhattan. She never married but has a son who I have only met once. We only send Christmas cards. Not very close. She is much younger, and we hardly knew each other growing up. Our mother died when she was six, and she had a difficult time as a young child. She probably fell in love with the first man who dated her. She has never told me about her relationship or pregnancy."

"What about your father?"

"He was always a drunk ever since I can remember. He died about twenty years ago. I didn't go back for his burial. Just didn't feel any emotional loss. He never exhibited any love, or even caring, for my mother. This is my apartment", she offered as she parked her Chevrolet in her assigned space.

"Have you always lived in an apartment?"

"Yes, I can't afford to buy in this neighborhood, and I don't want to be far from downtown. I can ride the bus and don't really need a car but like to take a drive to the country once in a while."

Jeffrey walked into the apartment feeling very uneasy. The sight of the living room couch, easy chair and television was disarming. Could he really sit there and relax without feeling the prying eyes of the other inmates and guards? That seemed an impossibility as a stranger in this woman's home. His strong impulse was to leave immediately without saying a word. Not even a thank you.

"Can I get you anything? I bought you some beer."

Her offer cleared his uneasiness considerably but not entirely. A beer would be relaxing, he decided, and he did really want sex before he left: plus, he didn't have anywhere to go.

"Yes, a beer would be good. Where should I sit?"

"Wherever you would be most comfortable. This is your home for now. I know it must feel strange and no doubt very different than your home before prison."

That comment did ease his discomfort. Without having thought about it, his mental perception of leaving those steel bars and concrete had put him back in his home with his furniture, his books and his scotch. He hadn't envisioned comfort in a different setting. It struck him as extremely unsettling that he hadn't been thinking rationally. Of course, he was going to feel strange in an unfamiliar situation. He was never going back to the home he had left where he was surrounded by his personal creature comforts. It was past time to wake-up to reality. He was now a different person, living a different life. He must decide how to live this new beginning. He must decide who the new Jeffrey Morris would be. As the realization hit him, his anger and mental anguish began to diminish. He was shocked by the relaxation that he was experiencing. It felt very good. A feeling he hadn't been in touch with since before his arrest. As he settled into the easy chair, beer in hand, the kind woman looking at him appeared more attractive. She was providing this outpouring of caring which he, all of a sudden, recognized as more than just good fortune. She didn't deserve to be the recipient of his anger. It wasn't her fault he had been framed.

14

Georgio's wasn't very busy on a Monday night. James was sitting in a secluded booth and looked anxious as Connie slid in.

"It looked like you were packing today, were you?"

"Yes, I am moving my store uptown. I got an offer I couldn't refuse, as the expression goes."

"How did that happen?" he responded.

Connie thought he was too interested in her personal life and replied: "I am here to talk about Robert, Jr., not me. If I agree, how do you plan to meet him?"

"He hangs out at a pool hall, and I intend to shoot with him."

"Where is the pool hall?"

"Connie, please don't be offended but I don't want you to know. I don't want you ever, for any reason, going to that pool hall. It wouldn't be good for Robert, Jr. or you. If you knew the location, you might be tempted to feel the need at some time to find him, and I can't let that happen. It is too dangerous".

"How do you plan to get Robert, Jr. out of that gang?"

"Through his passion for pool. He is very good, and I am pretty decent myself. I am going to offer to sponsor him and I as doubles partners in big money games uptown, and then in other cities. If I get him traveling out-of-town, he will eventually lose contact with the gang. The 'high' of winning, if we can win and the good money will overpower the gang influence."

"How long will it take?"

"Probably a few months, I can't rush it or it will seem not natural."

"How do you know he is a good pool player?"

"I have watched him play a few times while I have been sitting at the bar. He never loses. I will challenge him to a game and give him good competition which he rarely enjoys."

"I never knew you played pool."

"I didn't until I went to China. My dad played and he taught me. We played in big money games as partners. It was Robert, Jr.'s grandfather's passion, as well. He pedaled cars during the day and played pool nearly every night."

"Was your father re-married?"

"Yes, they had a son, but they were separated as he never spent any time with her."

"What about your mother? Where does she live?"

"She died while I was in China, and I wasn't able to come back for the funeral. She didn't know if I was alive or dead, just as you didn't."

Could Robert, Jr. be arrested now?"

"Yes, I am almost certain he could. I talked to one of his gang members at the bar that had too much to drink, and he said some suspicious things. It is possible he was just inflating his ego, but it sounded real to me."

Connie offered: "I think I saw that woman at the bar looking at you. Do you know her?"

He looked right at Evelyn without any change in facial expression, and said, "No, I don't."

"Go ahead with your plan. I am leaving and that woman will undoubtedly be glad I did."

Robert replied, "I would like to walk you to the subway."

"No, that is not necessary, and I certainly don't want to disappoint that woman", she said with indignance.

James thought it sounded like jealousy although Connie was certainly showing no interest in him. Her feelings of twenty-two years ago were non-existent. As she left, she stopped at the bar and said something to the woman on the bar stool and departed quickly. James was very curious and went immediately to the bar stool.

"Do you know the woman who just spoke to you?"

"No, I have never seen her before."

"What did she say to you?"

She said: "He is all yours now".

"Were you looking at me while we were sitting in the booth?"

"Perhaps. Is she your girlfriend?"

"No, she isn't. Just a business interest."

15

James walked into Mei Lin's dry-cleaning and upstairs to her apartment. He knocked on the door and said: "Are you home, Auntie?"

"Yes, James. Come in. Connie OK with Robert, Jr. plan?"

"She is onboard and, hopefully, the ship leaves dock tonight. If Robert, Jr. is at the pool hall, I intend to beat him in three consecutive games. He is very good but has a flaw which I can correct. He only thinks one shot ahead, not three shots: including his opponent's shot. I can get his attention when I beat him. He has beaten me each time we have played, and he will realize that I have been toying with him and wonder why. After proposing our partnership, I will tell him about his flaw."

"What if offer not interest him?"

"It will. It is his only passion, not even thoughts of girls or boys share his singular interest. When is Connie moving in?"

"Sunday. I send truck to her store and apartment and Alice apartment, too: She is coming, also."

"Speaking of girls, I met a woman last night at the bar. I'm going to see her again."

16

Connie called Evelyn later on Monday night hoping she was home and not with James.

Evelyn answered, "No, I am alone. I knew what you were going to ask."

"Well, did you meet him?"

"Yes, I was stunned when you came to the bar stool. Your message was very repeatable: very clever. Robert came over immediately and asked if I knew you. I am certain he doesn't know we are friends. Telling him I was looking at him was brilliant. It motivated him to show an interest; otherwise, I doubt he would have. Didn't strike me that he was the aggressive type. He told me he recently moved here from Chicago and plays pool for a living. No mention of China. We are going to meet for drinks on Saturday night. I have another date with George on Friday. Told James my Friday's are already committed to keep his competitive spirit intact."

"He must be very competitive if he plays pool for a living: quite different than a construction worker. That profession must me infested with lots of scum. I would never tell anyone that is how I made a living; not very appealing to a woman."

"I thought James Whitmore looked a little Asian. Did you think that?"

"Yes, he said he had his plastic surgery done in China."

"That fits, the pool playing also fits but Chicago does not. If he is from Chicago, he lied to me. That would mean he is not Robert Young. Let's see if he tells us any other different stories. Chicago and pool playing fits with the crooks and the gang life. I gave him the OK to meet Robert, Jr. and play pool with him. I hope he gets back to me soon. He wouldn't give me his address or phone number: very suspicious. Did you get it?"

"No, I didn't ask but I will on Saturday. How did the packing go today? Could you use some help?"

"Sure, come over any night. The truck comes on Sunday."

17

Freedom Flight

"Jenny."

He surprised himself when he heard his voice call her by name.

"The pictures: they are not you, are they"?

"No, I knew my pictures would not excite you the way you wanted to be excited. They are pictures I took of a woman who is a friend of my sister's in New York. I met her when I visited there six years ago. We became very conversive and still write occasionally. She is very pretty and has a gorgeous body. I know you are disappointed to look at me. I don't expect you to lust for me the way you must have lusted for her. If you don't want me, my feelings are not hurt. I am quite familiar with being unnoticed."

"Which direction is your bedroom?"

She was excited as she lifted herself from the sofa and placed his left hand in hers. Then she put it lightly on her large right breast and smiled slowly and enticingly. Her femininity generated his immediate increased blood flow. As he stood up, his right hand commenced caressing that beckoning leg. His hand quickly moved under her short skirt and to her ass. He pressed his hard masculinity into her body. She felt his large penis rubbing against her already wet deep valley. The porn she had watched had also made her wet. She relished the change in her body. His left hand had located her very accessible cleavage and he massaged her right nipple with excessive vigor. She desperately wanted him to kiss her and feel his tongue in her mouth, but he made no effort to pursue that sexual arousal. His strong arms lifted her, and he carried her directly to the bedroom shower.

As he slid the shower door, she said: "Shouldn't we undress?"

He didn't answer as he turned on the water. Both became soaked immediately and her hard nipples were now protruding through her shear blouse as the bra had been unhooked. He dropped his pants and briefs and put her hand around his already pulsating organ. He moved her hand to begin stroking his very large masculine tool while he continued to massage both nipples through her drenched blouse. He put her other hand around his balls and moved it in rhythm to her right hand. The movies and books had not prepared her for this; nevertheless, he seemed to be getting what he wanted. She now wanted that big, hard masculinity in her valley but apparently that wasn't going to happen right now. Very quickly, sooner than she expected, he erupted in her hand.

"Keep stroking", he muttered and exhaled with relief. He didn't say anything and just took the bar of soap to begin bathing his entire body while her hands remained engaged. She was shocked with disappointment. Was this all he wanted? Did he not have any desire to give her pleasure? The pictures had worked for him but were a disaster for her. His tongue had not tasted her breasts.

Within minutes, her soft stroking hands had generated another "hard-on."

"Put that big boy in your mouth and give me tongue."

The shower floor was hard on her knees; however, not nearly as hard as he was. He put his hands behind her and pulled her head in and out of his masculinity.

She exited the shower and disrobed her wet clothes. They were drenched in semen and went immediately to the washer. After dressing, she exited to the other bathroom to vent her disappointment. The tears washed away her desire of a first climax. She felt raped again: a feeling she had been trying to forget for thirty-five years.

As her overpowering emotional low slowly dissipated, Jenny emerged from the bathroom to find Jeffrey gone: no note or sign of his departure. She felt mixed emotions: relief that her disappointment would not reoccur and her concern that her dreams of developing a love relationship had vanished. Her mind was in disarray. Her life, at this moment, was void of direction. She couldn't even decide her next mental or physical movement. Inertia didn't exist. She literally was motionless. It was a feeling that was foreign to her. Maybe she was suffering a mental break-down, she pondered. It seemed like hours, but it was probably only a few minutes when Jeffrey re-entered her home.

"I went out for some fresh air. Our time in the shower was so pleasurable: I just wanted to walk and relish the sensation. Your feminine touch erased some very disturbing memories. I apologize for my selfishness. I know I didn't provide any pleasure for you. I really needed to experience a woman's touch to release my inhibitions. I was raped several different times in the prison shower and am concerned I may have been exposed to venereal disease. I wouldn't take the chance of carrying that infection to anyone else by engaging in intercourse."

Jenny's panic-stricken mental state evaporated when she listened to Jeffrey's explanation of his behavior. He really was conflicted and for good reason. His expressed concern of being a sexual disease carrier confirmed her expectations of his positive character values. However, she silently wondered if oral sex could transmit venereal disease.

She responded by impulse: void of any thought process: "I will make a Doctor's appointment for you right now to address your concerns. If you have contracted any disease, you can certainly be cured or treated. In the meantime, we can get in the shower together anytime you wish."

"Thanks for understanding. It may take a while for me to pleasure you, and I do want to do that. You deserve it."

As never before, Jenny was surprisingly motivated to discuss her personal inhibitions. She had never heard another person say to her that they had been raped.

"I also was raped by two boys when I was sixteen. I have been afraid ever since to engage in sex. I don't know if I can have pleasure. I do know you are the first man I have met that has aroused my interest in finding out. I am a virgin as I have never experienced an orgasm. Maybe it is too late, but I want to try, and you are the man I want to give me my first sexual pleasure, if that is possible."

Jeffrey was aroused again. The thought of pleasuring a fifty-five-year-old virgin was very stimulating. The phony pictures were no longer visible in his mind. Jenny was now the object of his sexual drive. He wanted to hear her groan and see her facial expression when she first felt her feminine release. He wanted to be "the man" who gave her an orgasm.

"I certainly hope I am clean and can be the man you have been anticipating. Your long-awaited expressed desire has given me another erection. Let's go to the shower again."

"Let's go to the bedroom. My knees don't need that shower floor again."

Jeffrey almost exploded in his pants as he heard her suggestion. Fortunately, he was able to constrain his physical impulse until her tongue had engulfed his hard and enlarged tool. At that moment, he wasn't able to constrain any longer. It was very quick, too quick, and he was a little embarrassed.

"In time, I will be able to control my desire to climax; I will need your patience"

This time, her tongue and lips had savored the taste. She thought it felt like nothing she had ever imagined. Her nipples got hard, and her pleasure was on the verge of total ecstasy. She was certain if she did incur a venereal disease, the treatment would be worth it. She wasn't going to miss out any longer on this pleasure. Not even one day. The next time she anticipated his penetration at her urging and crossing "the verge" threshold. The Doctor's exam results would not be a barrier. She had waited too long to be "womanized."

18

Robert Jr. wasn't at the pool hall on Tuesday night, nor were his "buds". That concerned James, and he casually asked the bartender: "Where is everybody? No one to shoot pool with."

"I think they go dancing on Tuesdays at Sammy's on Sixth Street. I heard they have free drinks for the girls on Tuesdays. I hear them talking about the girls they meet there. Sounds like they have a good time."

James wanted to go to Sammy's to see if Robert Jr. had joined them but knew he shouldn't as it would look like he was following them: better to take it slow.

"That is Pete, the owner, sitting at the end of the bar. He might want to shoot with you. He likes to play for a little money but doesn't usually play with his customers. He doesn't want to take their money. Would you like me to ask him?"

"Sure," was James's answer.

The owner accepted the invitation, as unbeknownst to James, he wanted to vet him.

"Hello James, I have seen you playing, and you are quite good. I don't think I can give you a game. Give me a 2-ball handicap and we will play for $20. If I win, we will eliminate the handicap on the second game, and you can get your money back. You break as I have two balls of my choice after the break in the pocket."

James agreed and promptly ran the table. Pete didn't get a shot.

"Pete, you break and get a 4-ball handicap. Chance to get your $20 back."

Pete smiled and said: "I've seen enough: keep the dough. I will buy you a beer. Where did you learn to shoot like that?"

"I have been playing since I was six years old. My father taught me. It was his passion."

"Where does he live?"

"He died about three years ago: smoked all his life. The big 'C' got him."

"I'm sure you miss him. Did you live near him before he died? Were you able to spend much time with him?"

"Yes, we both lived in Chicago and visited every week."

"Do you have children?"

"One son but I don't get to see him. Circumstances created our separation."

"Does he live in Chicago?"

"I am not certain where he lives."

"Other than shooting pool, what fills up your life? Are you married?"

"Not any longer."

"Have a girlfriend?"

James was beginning to think Pete was asking too many questions. However, it was in his interest to bond with Pete. Being accepted as a "regular" at the pool hall would get him closer to Robert Jr.

"No girlfriend but I am pursuing one."

"What is your line of work?"

"I sold new cars in Chicago."

"What brought you to New York?"

This was James's chance to join the underworld.

"Some of the money buying the cars was dirty, and the law was getting close to me."

"Do you plan on looking for that line of work in New York? If you do, I might have a contact for you."

"I might but not just yet. I'm involved in another project right now."

"Let me know when you are ready."

"Thanks for the offer."

Pete wasn't sure about James, but he had the ball rolling.

19

Robert, Jr. and his "buds" were in Hartford. The plan was identical except for the Penske truck. However, the result was considerably different. The RE/MAX realtor arrived during the burglary with a prospective buyer. Robert Jr. alerted the window guard of the impending danger, and the gang fled the scene. It was very close to a disaster. In fact, the RE/MAX car passed the Exit Realty vehicle on the street about 100 yards from the driveway. Robert Jr.'s phone call prevented their discovery. Had he not observed that a RE/MAX car was heading in the direction of the burglary in progress and recognized the possibility of a surprise visit, the criminal activity would have been a face-to-face encounter. To Robert Jr.'s knowledge, no one in the gang carried a gun, thank Goodness. Burglary was one thing: murder was a whole "nother" world. As he drove the semi back to Manhattan, the "closeness" was all he could think about. The safety element in the plan had worked. However, he now knew that it wasn't flawless. The thought of going to prison was extremely concerning but didn't compare to the pain it would cause his mother. Until now, he always thought the plan would prevent him from ever being caught now he wasn't sure.

Robert Jr. returned to the pool hall on Wednesday evening. He had called his mom and told her he was back from tubing. When he arrived, he joined his "buds" at the table. He always gave them heavy handicaps and still prevailed. They had a bet among themselves regarding who would be the first one to beat him. James came in about an hour later and was relieved to see him: he wasn't in jail yet. The opening developed in short order when Robert Jr. achieved victory. James put his money on the table as the next challenger. A $20 purse with no handicap. The game wasn't close: James ran the table on his second shot. Robert Jr. made the mistake of leaving him a set-up table. James won two more close games. He wanted to beat Robert Jr. but not humiliate him. The next challenger picked up his $20 bill and said, "That is a game I don't know."

James addressed Robert Jr., who was very dejected: "Let me buy you a beer. I took advantage of a flaw in your game. Would you like to know what it is?"

Robert Jr. couldn't refuse. He wanted to know what James had to say.

"Robert, Jr. I would like to meet you here when the 'buds' are gone. I want to show you what I observed in your game. In return, I have a proposal I would like to offer you."

Robert Jr.'s intrigue was peaked.

"Let's go to the First Street pool hall now and you can tell me."

"I would rather not. I don't want anyone to see or hear us."

Now Robert, Jr. was beside himself with eagerness.

"Is 10:00 tomorrow morning OK with you?"

"I will be here."

James went immediately to Pete and asked: "I would like to rent the pool room at 10:00 tomorrow morning. What would it cost?"

"Depends on why you want it."

"I want to give a pool lesson for an hour. Nothing illegal."

"I guess $300 would cover it. There are only a couple of drunks here at that time anyway. I will put a 'Closed' sign on the door."

"I need you to keep it silent: no one should know why you're closed."

Pete found that mysterious but agreed. He intended to be watching what was taking place from the back room anyway. Maybe this James was more interesting than he previously thought.

James knew Pete was ripping him off, but it was cheap if his proposal was successful. He told Robert, Jr. that he arranged with Pete for them to have the pool hall to themselves.

"See you in the morning."

James called Connie immediately and told her the plan had been implemented.

20

Freedom Flight

"We have a blood test at the Doctor's office on Tuesday, Jeffrey". The nurse said it would take at least two weeks to get the results. If we do have any disease, the treatments will be on-going for months. Have you given any more thought about what you would like to do to re-engage your life with society?"

"Yes, but nothing has emerged. I have been walking the pavement observing people living their lives: wondering what motivates each of them to appear to be so intent to pursue their purpose. Most of them are hurrying to get somewhere. I never thought much about other people's lives but now it monopolizes my thoughts."

"Jeffrey, why don't you ask them?"

"What do you mean?"

"Hearing their answers would give you some peace. Your curiosity would be satisfied and perhaps provide some direction for you. Your intelligence and education would provide you the opportunity to evaluate their activity and compare it to your own obscure interests. Something may blossom as you study others. At the very least, your mind will be exercising, and I know you like that."

"People might be offended if I asked them personal questions."

"Some people yes, and you can apologize to those who are. I think most people like to discuss their lives if they are approached with a sincere interest. If you initially impress them as honestly seeking their help, I believe most will be helpful. The challenge will be to impress them with an honest approach; as otherwise, they would see you as a con man trying to take advantage of them. That challenge will certainly help you assimilate into society once again. You will be using the same skills that elevated you to a position of Vice-President."

Jeffrey was silent as he considered Jenny's counsel. Her suggestion would involve utilizing considerable psychology in order to secure a stranger's trust. He did harbor some degree of confidence that he possessed skills in effective communication. His ability to engage strangers had generated his success in the banking business. The more he thought about it, the more intrigued he became.

"I like your idea. I could go to the park and start talking to people who return my eye contact and greeting and move on to coffee shops or lunch counters. I could keep notes and analyze similarities: a study in socialization. Perhaps, I could even write a book. The idea is stimulating, even exciting…contrasting prison life to the human nature that exists on the sidewalks of life."

"That even sounds like a book title. Your excitement makes me excited! Can I be your sounding board as you write? I would like to give you my reaction to your written words."

"Certainly! Your insight to help improve my mental health generated our excitement. We can be a partnership in this endeavor."

Hearing that word gave Jenny a serene composure. "Partnership" was her objective. Perhaps the bedroom was not the only place she could provide his satisfaction. Her longing to be important in his life was becoming a reality after all these years. It was almost surreal that her fantasy might come to life. Was the universe going to provide a fulfilling realization after all? She wasn't certain she deserved it, but she was eager to accept it.

21

Alice was packing boxes without help. Her parents had been deported a year earlier. Her younger brother had been murdered only six months ago. It had been a very unpleasant year, and she had shared her grief with Connie. At times, she thought about returning to the Philippines to join her parents. Not having any close friends, except for her boss Connie, was a lonely life. She made good grades in high school and graduated with honors. College was not a possibility as her applications for total financial aid had not been answered. She would dearly like to improve her standard of living but did not have the resources to seek a position in one of those tall buildings. Although an attractive girl, her very low economic status was obvious by her attire. Even with the employee discount when selling new clothes, she couldn't afford to purchase those. At Connie's shop, she occasionally got a free dress when the owner didn't return to pick it up. She was hopeful that closing the shop might be a bonanza as some women could not be reached or didn't respond to her phone calls. In the new uptown store, she was excited to get one of those dresses to go out in the evening. She would like to meet a young man; however, working in a women's' shop didn't provide much of an opportunity for that. A hair stylist or nail salon was far beyond her reach. "Dress for success" prohibited her pursuit of an office position.

She had a boyfriend in high school for about three months. She wasn't in love with him; however, his company was enjoyable. He made her laugh and took her to some friends' parties. Drug use was the theme of the gatherings and Alice had no interest. Her brother, two years younger, was addicted to heroin and it consumed his life and, eventually, contributed to his death. She thoroughly enjoyed the boyfriend's kisses; however, when his hand reached between her legs, the enjoyment ceased. Her strict Catholic upbringing prevented any thought of sex before marriage. He found her prudish beliefs very unrealistic, and the dating ceased quickly. She had decided that all boys expected sex, and therefore, romance was not in her "picture". How do you ask a boy when you first meet him if he is willing to wait for marriage before having sex? Otherwise, when he expects to receive sexual satisfaction, the short-lived companionship terminated: What was the point...only disappointment.

22

Robert Jr. was right on time which was his normal routine. James had already arrived, and the balls were racked. Pete put the "Closed" sign on the door and exited to the back room. The private setting was in place, and James commenced the conversation. He explained the flaw, and they proceeded to play. Robert Jr. got the message immediately.

"Robert, Jr., you can be a prosperous pool shark. Twenty-dollar games are beneath your potential. I would like you to be my partner in big money games. I will put up the $5,000 per man entrance fee and, in turn, split the earnings 80/20. If we don't win, I lose $10,000. If we win, you can pocket $20,000. There are 10 teams in a tournament. We alternate shots. If I run the table, you shoot first in the next game. A flip of the coin determines which team breaks. It is a best of five series, and the loser goes home. Do you think you have the nerve to play under that pressure?"

"How often do we play?"

"Two Saturday nights per month."

"Can we play this Saturday?"

"Yes, but I want us in a $1,000 game to see how you handle it."

"How do you know about these games?"

"I played in them with my father in Chicago before he passed."

"Did you win often?"

"Most of the time."

"Was he better than me?"

"Yes, but he had been playing for many years. I have been looking for a partner since his death: Tried three, actually, but never won. It is winner-take-all so I lost a lot of money. Some of our opponents are not that good but they are rich, and their egos keep them coming back to lose. There are always two or three quality opponents. Don't expect to win every time but if we don't win after six entries, we will need to abandon the plan."

"I know it is not my business but where do you get all that money you lose?"

"My father was rich, and we made a lot more money playing pool."

"I think 20 percent is not enough as your partner. If we win one of the first three events, I want 30 percent."

"Your negotiating skills are good. You have it. Let's practice."

23

James arrived early at Georgio's on Saturday. Fifteen minutes after scheduled, Evelyn had not showed. Finally, ten minutes later, she walked in.

"Did you hope I would get tired of waiting and leave?"

"No, just wanted to see if I was worth waiting for".

"Well, I guess I don't know that yet. Tell me what you want to drink and then I want to hear about your life."

"I will have Merlot. There's not much to tell. I have always lived in Manhattan. My father was a doorman at the Hilton. He raised four kids after my mother died. I have never traveled other than a few trips to New Jersey. My husband was a 'dirty' cop. He got caught and went to prison. I divorced him while he was locked up and haven't heard from him since. What about you? Are you married?"

"Not now. I was once and have a son."

His interest in her was accelerated when Connie spoke to her when leaving the restaurant. Her explanation was reasonable: "He is all yours now." Evelyn had admitted that she may have glanced at him a couple of times and volunteered that he had an interesting and handsome face. The handsome part had motivated him to ask for this date.

"Are you close to your son?"

"No, we haven't spoken in probably six years now."

"If I'm not being too personal: what happened?"

He interpreted the question as his opening to qualify her interest.

"If personal is what you need to begin a relationship then ask me anything. My son was caught stealing cigarettes from a grocery store. He was carrying a gun when he was caught and received a sentence of six years. I've tried to see him, but he refuses: won't answer my letter, either."

"Sorry I made you explain that."

Evelyn's voice turned soft and warm for the first time. James liked the change.

"You mentioned a relationship: what does that mean to you?"

"Dinners, movies, quiet romantic nights watching TV."

"Does it lead to living together or do you not want that commitment?"

"Commitment is great if the compatibility is there. I don't like arguing and won't live that way."

"Two people don't always agree on everything", Evelyn responded.

"That is true. However, they don't need to argue. They can resolve the issue with rational discussion."

Evelyn was very impressed: this man sounded intelligent and educated.

"Where did you go to college? she asked.

"I didn't."

"Your vocabulary sounds like you did."

"I do a lot of reading: self-educated, I guess."

"Thanks for the wine." How do we move forward from here?"

"I think we spend as much time together as possible and hopefully our comfort with each other will grow. Would I be offending you by suggesting I want to move beyond compatibility as soon as possible? You are a beautiful woman, and my hormones are already flowing."

Evelyn thought: that answers the question. Connie is not his objective. He is showing too much interest in me, and I am certainly interested in him.

"Well, you will have to take a cold shower because we are not going to my apartment tonight."

"I didn't expect that we were. If we decide to have a relationship, I don't want it to be built on only lust. However, the sooner we can get to lust the better for me. Are you available on Wednesday evening for a movie date? Do you like movies?'

"Some movies."

"You pick this movie, and I will pick the next one."

"James, you are much more than I expected: Either that or your 'line' is near perfect. I hope it isn't a 'line' and only time will tell. I will pick the movie."

"I am not giving you a 'line' and the sooner you accept that, the closer we are to a relationship. May I have your address and pick you up?"

"Of course."

24

Pete called his friend in Chicago who also owned a pool hall.

"Hello, John. This is Pete in Manhattan. I need some information. Check on a guy who calls himself James Whitmore. He is in his forties and is an excellent pool player. Claims to be from Chicago and sold new cars by moving dirty money; says the law was moving in."

"I will ask around: doesn't sound like anyone I know. I heard your Hartford business had a near miss. Have you made any changes to prevent it from happening again?"

"Yes, I sent you a note by courier; apparently you don't have it yet."

"Now, this James Whitmore, does he pose an interference?"

"He concerns me—too polished: his vocabulary is too good for a pool bum. Could be he is educated and just prefers to be unconnected from the skyscrapers."

Pete had approached Robert Jr. and asked him what James had discussed with him. When he heard the details of the offer, he asked: "How does he know where these big money games are located in Manhattan since he only recently moved here?"

"I didn't ask him."

"Find out. I know you are close-mouthed but watch what you tell him. He concerns me: could be undercover law, or he could be who he says he is. Either way, I am glad you are partnering with him. We can keep a better eye on him with your close contact. Find out all you can and get his address and phone number. He said he is interested in a woman. Find out who she is."

25

Freedom Flight

Since becoming an integral part of Jeffrey's life. Jenny was enjoying life more than ever before. It had only been two weeks since he had put prison life in the rear-view mirror, and they were already living much like a normal couple. He had commenced with his personal interactions on the street, and he came home to her loaded with stories to share.

"I met a man today who had endured three years in prison. We compared our experiences, and they were very similar. He was convicted of insider trading and neither was he sentenced to reside in the 'country club', as other inmates labeled it. His Judge, as did mine, viewed his criminal activity as not worthy of the less violent incarceration. If we had received the good fortune of a more lenient Judge, we could have been spared the shower attacks. He has been 'out' for two years and still hasn't found white collar employment. He busses tables at the Rendezvous restaurant in the Hilton. Some of his 'regulars' have asked him about his life as they recognized his educated demeanor. He is hopeful that one of them may offer him an office position. However, none of them have. He is estranged from his wife and children and lives alone void of any socialization. His plight generates my appreciation of the good fortune you have provided me. I hope my book is published and lots of money comes pouring in; enough to pay my court ordered restitution and provide some adventures for you. Would you like to 'see the world' if you had the financial means?"

"I would only enjoy traveling if you were by my side. I hope my expression of feelings doesn't heighten your fear of being a captive again. I would never want to possess you, but I really hope to continue to share your life. I don't expect love in return, only companionship."

Jeffrey wasn't surprised by her utterances as he was very aware of her devotion to his comfort. Her words confirmed her actions.

However, he was unsure how to respond so he didn't. Although he had developed a deep appreciation for Jenny's affection, he hadn't given any thought to his own emotional state of mind. In fact, he now realized that his callousness must be evident to her. He had an uncomfortable feeling of guilt. She didn't deserve that. She deserved compassion, at the very least. Silently, he vowed to express that sentiment often in the future.

"I had a phone call from the Doctor's office today. They want us to come in tomorrow for the results."

26

Before Evelyn called Connie, she had to get her mind right. Connie said she had no interest in James: that could change, and she didn't want anything to affect their friendship. James had made a seriously positive impression, and Evelyn knew she could fall for him. She had been disappointed when he didn't kiss her good night at the subway station on their first date. She definitely was also feeling lust. Beyond that, he might be willing to pay her rent: he said he didn't have any ties in New York. Briefly, she had a mental picture of making him poached eggs for breakfast following a wake-up orgasm. I wonder if he likes being devoured to "whet his appetite". Her fantasizing must stop, she thought, as Connie may rediscover her feelings for him if she becomes comfortable that he really is Robert Young: her son's father. He must be Robert Young—no other real possibility exists. I want him to be an imposter: that way, I can follow my feelings without guilt. His intelligence, understanding, and apparent openness make him very attractive. If he is just telling me what I want to hear, he has me pegged 100%. I better stop all this daydreaming and call Connie.

"Hello, Evelyn. I have been anxious to talk to you. James told me that he has approached Robert, Jr. and they plan to partner in pool. What did you learn?"

"Connie, this man is either the 'best catch' I have ever met, or the best pick-up artist ever invented. If we were not such good friends, I would have used every feminine wile to get him into my bed. He doesn't want to be intimate unless we have a committed relationship. No other man has ever told me that. I hope he is an imposter because I want him. I don't want Robert Young---your lover: I want James Whitmore. If and when I feel him inside me, I don't want to be thinking of you flying in the open sky. I want to have my own euphoria: whatever it is. Tell me to stop now before I let myself fall in love."

"Evelyn, I have already told you I have no interest in this man except his offer to help Robert, Jr. I don't know who he is or why he wants to help so you enjoy. I got you into this, and you have no obligation to me. The universe works in mysterious ways and seems to be blessing us both. Let's take it one day at a time and see how it develops for both of us. What about George?"

"George, I almost forgot about him! I think I will keep seeing him on Friday nights for now and enjoying the dinners and sex. Nothing may ever happen with James, but if it does, I will drop George---pronto. He doesn't want a commitment, only once a week sex. I asked him 'straight out" last Friday when he was most vulnerable."

"When was that?"

"When his 'hard-on' left my hand and his tongue left my mouth: if ever he was going to say yes to a commitment it would be then, even if he was lying. At least he was honest. He only responded: "Just enjoy what I am about to give you. Don't make me lose it". When he had exhausted himself the second time, he said: "Can we do this again next Friday?" And I said, "Why not until someone with a better tongue shows up and can do it three times. I wanted him to feel a little inadequate. He might try 'harder' next week to give me even more satisfaction."

"Evelyn, did you ever consider you might be nympho?"

"Oh, I am sure I am. Can't get too much of a good thing. When I was first married, we did it at least once a day and on the weekend at least twice a day. Despite wearing him out, he started 'sleeping around' with anything strange. I caught him several times, and he didn't deny it. He only justified it by saying: 'You can go out too; maybe, we can have some threesomes. Wouldn't you like two at the same time?' I divorced him a short time later: probably should have tried the threesome but I wasn't interested in having another woman in my bed. My tongue doesn't waggle in that direction."

"I am glad to hear that. I hope James Whitmore is ready. Every day might be too much to ask."

"I would be happy with twice a week if it was love and not just sex."

27

The truck arrived on schedule: first at Connie's and then at Alice's, and finally the store. One trip was enough as neither woman had much furniture. The store fixtures, mostly tables and racks, were folded up. Connie felt some sentiment as leaving a place she had spent nearly every day in for eight years was a loss. She had asked Robert, Jr. if he could help with the move. He said he would stay Saturday night and help finish the packing and offered to bring a rental truck. Connie said the truck had already been arranged. They had their best conversation in a long time during the packing. He even told her that he was going to play in some pool events for money. She asked if he could lose a lot, and he said: "Don't worry. I met a man who wants to sponsor me."

"What do you know about this man? Are you sure he is safe?"

"He is from Chicago and seems very safe: not like a gangster if that is what you mean."

"Can I come and watch you play?"

"No, mom, that isn't how it works. The games are usually in some rich guy's house, not public pool halls".

"Will you be able to spend more time with me when you start doing that?"

"Could be. I will have to see how much money I am making."

Connie had always found it strange that Robert, Jr. never visited her at the store. Now that he had agreed to go uptown today to the new location was most promising. Connie wondered if he thought it was safer and he wouldn't be seen.

When they arrived at Alice's apartment, Connie was glad to see that she lived comfortably. Her furniture wasn't soiled and worn out. She introduced Alice and Robert, Jr. and Alice said: "I have heard your name often: nice to finally meet you."

He appeared a little shocked as he reacted to her voice and only nodded. Connie was embarrassed that he didn't speak. She wanted to urge his greeting but thought better of it. The driver, Mei Lin's pick-up and delivery employee, helped carry furniture.

Robert, Jr.'s silence continued during the trip to the new location while the other three conversed continuously. The driver was a man in his late twenties and exhibited some interest in Alice. No wonder as her long black hair and dark skin were striking. Alice was polite but not personal as she had no interest in the man.

Alice remained in her new apartment and directed the placement of furniture. While the other two were traversing down the stairs, Robert Jr. blurted out: "Do you like that guy?!"

His body language and raised voice exhibited contempt. Now Alice was shocked and asked: "I don't even know him. Why do you ask?"

Had he not been Connie's son, she would have been offended. She didn't want to cause a problem with Connie.

"Because I like you."

His approach was cruder than any line a guy had ever given her, and she had heard a few. She wasn't sure how to reply and didn't.

"Will you go out with me?"

She now realized that he was very uncomfortable with women: not crude. He needed an answer. She thought: a no would stop his asking, a maybe would stop him ever asking again. She found his discomfort interesting and said politely: "I would like that."

Immediately, his demeanor changed to relaxed. His awkwardness evaporated and he offered: "Do you like movies?"

"Yes."

"Let's go Wednesday night."

"OK, what are we going to see?"

"I don't know. You pick one."

"Should we tell your mom?"

"I don't care."

He had felt his competitive spirit come alive when he saw the driver flirting with Alice. He didn't know how to flirt: had never tried. He had watched his "buds" do it and thought they were acting foolish and unmanly.

As they continued to unload, he even managed to smile a few times when he looked at Alice, probably a few too many times, she thought, and hoped his hormones would not dominate his behavior when they went to the movies. His obvious awkwardness might manifest a problem. On the other hand, the softness she had witnessed might be very pleasant. If so, she could take the lead in their time together. She could even take his hand during the movie if she sensed his uneasiness. Perhaps he had never been on a date given his clumsy approach. She was a virgin, and he could be a "virgin-dater". If that be the situation, he might not expect sex as all the others had. The more she thought about it, the more interested she became. Being the teacher and not the oppressed student would be a pleasant change. She wanted to tell Connie about their date and ask her more questions about him. Maybe she could then understand why he was so uncomfortable when asking her out.

28

James was anxious for Wednesday night to arrive. Evelyn was more than anxious as she wanted their comfort level to grow in order to move on. If he didn't kiss her tonight, she would be depressed. She had never dated a man twice who didn't make a move in pursuit of the conquest. Then the scary thought occurred. When he kissed her, would she purposefully pet the bird on the back of his neck? She just couldn't answer that thought. Maybe it would be safer to leave the bird for later, if later became reality.

Evelyn was ready on time and remarked: "Hi James: I decided you passed the test on waiting for me."

James countered: "Is your interest sufficient to wait for me?"

"My patience is limited so don't make me wait too long."

Both knew they were not referring to arriving late for a date. Both were comfortable with flirtatious comments. A good signal for compatibility, she thought.

"What movie are we going to see?" he asked.

"'Three Billboards': I heard it has award nominations and revolves around a woman's revenge."

"Are you revengeful? Should I worry if I disappoint you?"

"If you ever disappoint me, I will destroy your manhood."

They both laughed as he purchased the tickets.

During the movie, they both reacted at the same time; apparently, they shared a sense of humor. They quietly lamented their feelings to each other when Mildred demeaned the midget. After the movie, James suggested drinks and dessert.

"What kind of dessert do you like: blonds or redheads?"

"Hair color has never been my primary focus as I am a leg man and always check those first."

"How do mine stack up?"

"Don't know yet, I haven't seen most of them. They do go beyond your knees, don't they?"

Evelyn couldn't resist the question and put his hand on her thigh. "Does that answer your question?"

James thought: I like her forwardness despite our agreement. It seems like her lust is racing ahead of our compatibility.

Evelyn thought: I could devour him right now and right here in this bar.

"That poor midget was a good guy and received no appreciation from Mildred."

"She was all toughness with little compassion for anyone. It is not a wonder that her husband left her. However, I seriously doubt he could be successful attracting that beautiful young girl. He had nothing going for him."

James replied: "I agree. It was a good movie although it had a number of unrealistic situations. I prefer to see things in a movie that I find believable."

They both felt at ease, relaxed and under no pressure to impress.

After two drinks, James suggested that he walk her to the subway.

"No compatibility developing yet?", she asked.

"Absolutely", he replied. "How about you?"

"Couldn't be more content with who you are, James. Why don't you ride the subway with me?

29

Freedom Flight

"Come in, and please sit down for this good and bad news".

Jeffrey's silent reaction was immediate: this guy acts like he is offering dessert after a fine meal. He must realize that the results will determine how we must live the remainder of our lives. Jeffrey's anger, which had been missing for weeks, came to the surface again.

"Doctor, just drop the comedy act and give us the results."

Jenny was struck by Jeffrey's outburst and impulsively blurted out: "Doctor, we have both been very anxious about this moment for some time and our nerves are frazzled. Please forgive our sensitivity."

The Doctor then adopted a serious tone and stated: "You both have venereal disease. The good news is it can be cured with injections over an extended period of time."

"What period of time?", Jeffrey questioned.

"Perhaps one year, or worst-case scenario, two. It varies with the individual. You will need to cease having both oral and sexual intercourse. Otherwise, one person may be cured and again be infected by the other. We won't be able to determine the continuing carrier, and it will significantly lengthen the process."

Jenny's mind raced to the effect of his words: no orgasm for two more years! That possibility was devastating. She had already waited far too long for the expected pleasure and wasn't willing to accept this sentence.

Jeffrey was disappointed. He wasn't surprised or devastated but had been hoping for a blessing. Even though Jenny had urged him to accept her desire for oral sex, he was still responsible for transmitting the disease. Once again, he was feeling guilty of being an unworthy man: would he ever feel good about himself again? His doubts made his anger uncontrollable, and he immediately rose from his chair and left the room.

Jenny followed: calling him back.

"Jeffrey, wait for me! Please, let's talk about this."

When she caught him, she grabbed his arm and saw the grimace on his face. His pain was apparent.

"I knew the chance I was taking. You had the strength to tell me about your concern. It was strictly my decision; you were only granting my request. It was your open heart that prevailed, not any malice."

Her voice was pleading and full of despair. Jeffrey was startled out of his anger by her expression. After a long silence, he finally spoke.

"What are we going to do? Those injections will be very expensive and likely painful. They will endure forever."

"Let's talk about it when we get home. We will sit down calmly and rationally with a glass of wine and decide together what we want to do. The important thing is for us to be there for each other when making our decision. As long as we share our fate, we can continue to enjoy our time together."

Jeffrey continued to be shocked by Jenny's caring. He didn't realize that anyone could be that devoted. It was the first time in his sixty years that he had ever heard such an expression directed to him. As loving as she was, not even his mother would ever utter that sentiment, He wondered why the universe was providing this refuge in his life. He hadn't given Jenny any reason to care for him, and yet she was willing to live happily with their plight. Maybe that was the reason he had been framed? The universe worked in mysterious ways, and perhaps it was Karma that Jenny should be a light in his life. What a bizarre plan the universe had created. At that moment, he sensed a commitment that previously had been an unknown. Was he in love? Was this what it felt like? It was not a familiar emotion. Neither of his two previous relationships had generated this heartfelt response. Perhaps that is why they were short-lived and neither produced a commitment to make the other person happy. As he stood in the Doctor's office hallway, all these thoughts were born in a flurry. It was a mind-blowing few seconds.

"Let's go home and have that drink you suggested.

30

Pete received a courier note from Chicago. It read: No one ever heard of this guy. I am sure he didn't play pool for big money in this town. Lying about who he was aroused suspicion in Pete's mind. No doubt he was bonding with Robert, Jr. to get information about the gang's activity: telling him to avoid James was now a priority. The "buds" were scheduled to leave for Allentown on Tuesday evening. He would need to talk with Robert, Jr. before they left.

"Robert, Jr., I got a report on your James Whitmore: he isn't who he says he is. Find out all you can about him: I think he may be undercover. If he is, I will need to take care of it. Don't tell him anything but lies about yourself. Let him think he is getting close. Win that pool event on Saturday."

Robert, Jr. was disappointed to get this news as he kind of liked the guy. Just confirms my belief: you can't trust anybody.

At 10 a.m. on Wednesday morning, the two vehicles drove by the RE/MAX sign. Robert, Jr. was standing guard on the street in his usual role. The heist went smoothly, and he drove into the Manhattan warehouse about 4 p.m. Now his mind was solely on his date. He met her as planned at the movie theater.

"What are we going to watch?" he asked after greeting her.

"It is titled, 'Three Billboards'---something", she responded.

"Have you opened the new store yet?"

"Not until next week."

"Do you like the new apartment?"

"It is very convenient to work. I am not sure about living in that neighborhood with all those rich people. Some of them look at me like I don't belong."

"Did you tell mom about us going to the movie?"

"Not yet, I wanted to wait until I get to know you better."

They sat silently during the previews which gave Alice a chance to reflect. Robert, Jr. seemed perfectly normal: a little abrupt but not aggressive in his tone. She found him an attractive man with beautiful green eyes.

After the movie, she suggested they go to a restaurant for coffee.

"I don't drink coffee, but I will have a Coke."

He walked into the restaurant ahead of her, and she decided his manners needed her attention. Probably no one had ever taught him how to properly escort a woman. He didn't have a father role model and, according to his mother, lived most of his life on the streets

"Robert, Jr., by the way, may I just call you Robert or do you prefer the Junior added?"

"I don't care. My mom always included the Junior, and I just started to introduce myself that way. I figured the junior sounded to her like I have a father."

"I prefer Robert and that will be our secret for now if that is OK with you."

"Sure".

"Where do you live?"

He knew these questions would be coming and didn't want to lie to his first date at age twenty-two.

"Alice, I don't want to lie to you, but I can't tell you right now. That may upset you and if you don't want to date me again, I understand."

"Robert, I like you and want to see you again, but I don't want to be involved with anyone doing anything illegal. If you can't answer my questions about your life within six months, I will need to stop dating you. If you decide you still like me, you will need to stop living on the streets and being secretive. You need to prefer me to the streets, and I am giving you lots of time to make that decision."

He just looked at her. He certainly hadn't expected that response.

"I will think about that."

"Fair enough for now", she replied.

"Can I walk you home?"

"Yes, if I can hold your hand while we walk."

As they walked, she asked if he liked the movie.

"I liked Mildred. She was tough but I didn't like that cop. He should have been jailed for attacking that kid."

"Well, in real life, he would: movies are usually unrealistic. Living in jail would be a terrible life; nothing is worth that risk."

Her comment served its intended purpose. Robert didn't respond.

31

Connie was exhausted every night while completing the move… too tired to even relax with her usual two glasses of Merlot. Tired as she was, she did wonder what had happened that Wednesday evening with Evelyn's date. She hoped she would call soon. At 11 P.M., she decided that Evelyn was probably in James's arms. At 11:30, the phone rang.

"Sorry to call so late. James just left."

"A little early for your date to leave, isn't it?"

"It wasn't my choice."

"What happened?"

"I invited him in; I was really wanting him to stay. He didn't respond but pulled me tight to his strong body and kissed me softly. The kiss became stronger until I thought my lips were going to burst. I felt him get 'hard' as he pressed me. Then he said: "Evelyn, I want to come in. I feel very comfortable with you in every way, but I want our first intimacy to be a forever memory, not just a screw. I want to spend the evening talking and kissing during the warm-up. Then I want to make love to you for hours while neither of us is under the influence. I want your memory of your first orgasm with me to be vivid, not cloudy. I want to take you to a nice hotel on Friday night and have dinner in our room. Does that appeal to you?""

"I was like lifeless with his suggestion and replied: 'How long is it until Friday?' He smiled and kissed me again before he walked off. It was difficult to walk into the house as my legs were weak. I felt no strength in my body at all. That was nearly an hour ago. I just now got enough strength to call you."

"Wow, if he is who he says he is, he has vastly improved his technique."

"It wasn't technique", Evelyn replied curtly. "It was real emotion. This man is all real and couldn't fake who he is."

"You better call George and cancel your Friday date."

"You're right. I hadn't even thought of that."

Connie hung up and realized that she wasn't tired any longer. Evelyn's experience was creating adrenaline within her. She was uncomfortable with the feeling. She asked herself: why do I feel this way?

32

Robert, Jr. had a lot to think about: his date with Alice, her ultimatum and the new feeling he experienced while he was with her. He liked her femininity and caring attention. He also thought about the Saturday pool event and James's apparent undercover identity. A week ago, his life had been uncomplicated and now he had a lot of decisions to make. The one thing he was sure about was what he was feeling when he was with Alice. He didn't want to lose this newfound experience. Maybe it will "wear off", he thought. Maybe she will keep pressuring me to change my lifestyle. Six months was a long time but look how his life had changed in just a week. Saturday night would be very important to his decision-making. Finding out if he could possibly make a living playing pool was paramount. James claimed he did, and Robert, Jr. was confident he could play as well as James.

They met at the pool hall and took the subway to an upscale neighborhood.

"How did you find out about this game?" Robert, Jr. queried.

"I played here a month ago."

"Did you win?"

"No, my partner couldn't take the pressure. He missed a 'bunny' shot which would have won the game. I knew I had to find a new partner."

It seemed to Robert, Jr. that James was intentionally trying to make him feel pressure. However, it wasn't working. His confidence prevailed. He had been in too many tight situations on the street and had always managed to escape unscathed.

"Six-ball in the side pocket", James verbalized as they approached a door man. There were four pool tables in the very large game room. James put up their $2,000 for a total purse of $20,000. They drew cards to determine which teams would sit out first. James and Robert, Jr. would be watching. They were pleased to be able to observe the competition. None of the teams were dominant. James and Robert, Jr. never lost a game. There were not any introductions or socializing, only absolute focus by each player. When Robert, Jr. put the $6,000 in his pocket, he thought: this is more enjoyable than standing guard and driving a truck. It won't put me in jail, either. It could solidify my relationship with Alice. However, it won't last when Pete gets finished with James. He hoped James would continue so he could win $15,000 per event in the near future.

On the return trip home, Robert, Jr. spoke first: "That was great! Do you think we can win the $5,000 events?"

"I know we can if you continue to shoot like you did tonight."

"When can we play next?"

"If you are available, there is a game in Chicago in two weeks."

"What night of the week?"

"Always Saturday night."

"I am available."

"I will get us flight tickets for Saturday morning. We will need to stay over on Saturday night."

"Not a problem James but I need to ask you some personal questions."

"Shoot."

"It is obvious that you know your way around the pool halls in lots of cities. You must have connections to get into these events. I don't need to know about that, but I do need to know why the pool players in Chicago don't know you."

"What makes you say that?"

Robert, Jr. had decided he wanted to continue being James's partner and needed to warn him.

"Pete had you checked out and believes you are undercover law. Your life could be in danger."

"Not to worry. You just quit your gang life and keep winning at pool. I have a handle on Pete."

"What do you mean?"

"Can't explain it just now except you don't have to be concerned about me but I really appreciate that you are."

Robert, Jr. went to the campground and thought he might soon be moving to his mother's apartment. The feeling of not being secretive was enticing. Maybe the world was finally sending him some good fortune. The lack of which, he had always blamed on his disappearing father. James seemed very confident, but he wondered what the "handle" he had on Pete might be.

33

James phoned Connie on Sunday morning and told her that Robert, Jr. was seriously thinking about leaving the gang.

"How did you do that?"

"I can't say Connie, but we are bonding well. We won our first pool engagement. Robert, Jr. has good money in his pocket and realizes he might not need the 'buds'."

Connie wanted to ask him about his feelings for Evelyn but, of course, she couldn't. She did feel a spark of envy when thinking of the two of them together. She was overwhelmed with joy that he was bonding with his son and motivating him to leave the gang life. Not having any feelings for her ex-lover was confusing. She thought: twenty-two years is a long time, and I guess we both have changed a lot. I do feel a loss as he said our time together was the best of his life: mine, too. It won't be easy, but I will make myself be happy for them if they make each other happy. I wonder if he will be upset when he finds out Evelyn and I are close friends: like sisters.

James called Mei Lin: "I miss being able to visit with you."

"Me, too. How you do with Robert, Jr.?"

"Very well. Hopefully in a few months we can all visit together. The woman I met is very special."

"Good for you, you do good work - get reward."

"Have you heard from my father lately?"

"No word."

"You know I would like to contact him if I could.

34

Freedom Flight

Jenny and Jeffrey were both silent and introspective during the fifteen-minute ride home from the Doctor's encounter. After pouring the drinks, she expressed her feelings with a caring smile.

"It is nice to be surrounded by our own cozy place rather than that cold and sterile environment at the medical building, don't you think? Jeffrey, I want us to live a normal life… a life where we take solace in each other. You writing your book and me helping in any way I can to make each day one that makes you feel glad to be alive. I would like us to be a couple in every way. I have wanted that ever since I first saw you walking into the bank branch. You didn't know I existed behind that small window. I kept telling myself that someday we would be together. It required 36 years for that dream to be fulfilled. Now I don't want anything to alter my dream. Regardless of our illness, I want all of your body and mind enjoying all of mine. I want sex every time you want it. I want total sex in every form you have ever fantasized. We will endure the injections as long as necessary while still making love with each other. I have already checked and found that my insurance will cover my treatment, and your VA coverage will pay for yours. Considering the joy of sharing our lives, getting the shots is nothing more than an inconvenience well worth its cost. We can recover together and share our mutual discomfort. I totally understand if you don't feel the same way, but I am asking you to try it one day at a time. You can leave anytime, of course, without any explanation. Just give me today, and if any tomorrow changes your mind, I will accept your decision without consequence."

Jeffrey could hardly believe his ears. He could never have imagined being on the receiving end of such selflessness. This woman only wanted him, a jailbird, to make her happy. He had read about that kind of love but never even considered that it could happen to him.

"Jenny, I can't say that I understand your commitment to my happiness, but I certainly no longer intend to ignore it. I feel like making love to you at this very moment, in this very room, with the very best I can muster."

He walked directly to her chair and lifted her above his head while inserting his head under her skirt. His tongue licked her panties and then his teeth bit her wetness lightly. He put her down behind the chair with her derriere facing his now exposed hard erection. With vigor, he pulled her panties down, lightly pushed her head over the chair and pulled her legs apart. His penetration was slow but forceful. Then his thrusting became more accelerated and deeper. His hands squeezed her cheeks as he pulled them apart to increase the opening for his large masculine tool.

Jenny was barely aware that her body was being pulled back and forth by his strong hands. She was only aware of his stiffness generating a first-time sensation. A sensation she had only previously imagined. She wanted the pleasure to last forever.

"Oh, yes, Jeffrey, don't stop ever. Give me more. Go faster and harder."

Jeffrey responded with enthusiasm: "Take it all, baby. Take it all, you want it, and I am going to give it to you."

He moved his hands to her breasts and pulled her more aggressively as he continued to repeatedly go deep into her canyon.

She felt the wonderful release, first hers and then his. It was as if she had jumped from a rock cliff into a beautiful blue sky… soaring with the birds endlessly.

"Oh, Jeffrey, it was even better than I imagined. How often can you do that to me?"

35

Evelyn went directly to the hotel when she left the salon on Friday. She didn't need a dress for dinner with the evening James had planned. In fact, she didn't apparently need any clothes whatsoever.

James had already arrived and opened the door handing her a red rose. She kissed him softly and then licked his lips with her wet tongue. He was dressed only in boxer shorts and she wanted them off. Before she could get to them, he held her hands behind her back and with his other hand massaged her bodacious breasts. He slowly popped the buttons of her blouse exposing her big brown nipples. She had removed her bra before leaving the salon. He lightly bit one breast while massaging the other. Her nipples were already pointed and hard with desire. She couldn't resist a low moan and struggled to free her hands. She put one hand inside his boxer shorts and, without thinking, the other around his neck. She was startled by the sensation of the expanded wings on the small bird.

After finishing dinner, they listened to music on the TV and kissed and licked until both their bodies were covered with the other's scent. They showered together and the water rushing over their skin invited a continuation of their mutual desire and, once again, they consummated their insatiable thirst for each other.

Evelyn wasn't certain she could tell Connie the details of their lovemaking. She had always provided details about her previous lovers, but this was different.

As Connie was adjusting a light shade early Saturday afternoon in the shop, the phone rang.

"Connie, may I come over to visit?"

"Of course. Do you have the address?"

"Yes, I will be there in a couple of hours."

"I hope you bring good news, see you soon!"

Evelyn climbed the stairs and lightly knocked on the door.

"Evelyn, is that you?"

"Yes."

"Come in. I am in the kitchen, lots of drawers and cupboards to clean and line with contact paper."

"Connie, I think I am in love. I am indebted to you for life."

Her voice was soft: not coarse, as usual.

"Evelyn, you have only been on two dates with him. You are confusing lust with love."

"No, Connie, I feel both equally strong. I also feel guilty of wanting to spend every possible minute with your son's father. Flying through the clouds with my arms expanded was the most beautiful feeling of my life."

Hearing those words affected Connie in a way she never expected. She paused for what seemed like forever to Evelyn.

"Have I hurt my best and dearest friend?"

Connie sighed and said: "I was almost hoping he wasn't Robert Young. I do envy you Evelyn but certainly do not resent you. I didn't think I missed that feeling of love any longer, as well as flying, but I do. I sense a loss that I haven't thought about in many years. Please, don't tell me about your love and flying in the future! I am glad you are so happy. Any news of Robert, Jr.?"

"James said he was going to Chicago next Saturday to be in a pool event with a new partner. I asked about his partner and he said that he was a good kid who had a rough time of it, and he hoped he could help him find his way."

"That makes me feel better. My loss is Robert, Jr.'s gain."

36

The pigeon landed gracefully on the Manhattan roof top that covered the pool hall. It was her roost and she ate ferociously. It had been a long flight. As he routinely did, Pete arrived a short while later with water and more feed. He took the note from his pet's ankle and it read: "I found a group that knows James Whitmore. He won a lot of money from them in a private game: they say he is very closed-mouthed and OK. No concern about the law."

Pete was relieved that he or Robert, Jr. didn't have a problem. He needed to tell Robert, Jr. before the big money game. The concern might put pressure on him. A different pigeon carried a note, reading: "Hartford mishap avoidable."

Robert, Jr. wasn't at the pool hall that night and Pete had no way to contact him…no address, no phone number. That was the way Robert, Jr. wanted it.

As he approached Alice's door, he saw his mother coming up the stairs from her new store. He didn't know if she knew that he was dating Alice.

"Hi, mom, I guess you are surprised to see me?"

"Pleased, but not surprised. Alice told me that you two had a movie date. She is my good friend, don't you hurt her."

"Mom, I just like being with her: I won't do anything that hurts her."

"Have a nice time. What are you doing tonight?"

"Going to dinner."

Alice was ready and greeted him: "Nice to know you are punctual. A woman doesn't like to be kept waiting. Some men say they will call you and you never hear from them. Please don't ever do that to me."

"I won't."

During dinner, Robert, Jr. asked about her life.

"My younger brother was murdered on the street. I think the murder involved drugs. We were very close, especially after my parents were deported. They came illegally when I was three and my brother only one year of age. After high school, I got a job selling women's clothes and then the store closed. My parents left just before the store closed. It was a terrible time for me."

"Are you still in touch with your parents?"

"Yes, they hope to return to the U.S. some day."

"Mom said you told her about our date. She called you a good friend. I don't have any, either. I know lots of guys but don't consider any of them friends. I just met a guy that wants me to partner in pool with him: "big money games.""

"Are you good at pool?"

"Pretty decent but so are the guys I will be playing against."

"How often do you play?"

"Nearly every day."

"I mean for big money."

"He told me a couple times a month. We will need to travel to other cities."

"That sounds expensive."

"He is paying all expenses, and I can make $15,000 when we win."

"Wow, that is a lot of money!"

"He is also paying the entry money until we start winning. Then I will have to pay my own way."

"I hope you have enough left over for movies and dinner."

"I will make sure of that", and he smiled." How often do you want us to date?"

"I think twice a week would be nice, don't you agree?"

"As often as you like," he responded.

When they got up to leave, he started to bolt ahead. She grabbed his arm and sat him back down.

"Robert, I don't want to offend you, but I need to walk in front of you when we come in and leave the restaurant. It makes a woman feel like a lady. Opening the door and letting her go first makes you a gentleman. Will you be my gentleman?"

"I want you to feel like a lady always when you are with me. If that makes you feel like a lady, then I am happy to do that."

When they reached her apartment building holding hands, she asked: "Would you like to give me a goodnight kiss?"

<h1 style="text-align:center">37</h1>

The store opened on Monday as scheduled. Shortly after 9:00 A.M., a florist truck arrived. The note was addressed: "To Mom and Alice: Congratulations, you both deserve it!"

The women looked at each other with admiration.

"I had no idea my son could be this thoughtful. It must be your influence."

"I hope you are right. I think he just needed a light to give him optimism. The goodness was always there. Connie, may I ask you some personal questions about Robert, Jr.?"

"Of course, you are my partner now."

Robert, Jr. kissed me good night at my invitation, and I felt a scar on the back of his neck. Is he sensitive about that?"

Connie was taken back and had never told anyone about his inheritance. Now she couldn't avoid her secret.

"He has never asked me about it", she responded. "You can ask him. It is a birth mark that his father had. Someday I will tell him, but he has never asked how he got the mark. Let me know how he reacts but please don't tell him that it is an inheritance. If you and my son continue to date and get serious, I will tell you more about his father. There are things he doesn't know."

Alice was very curious and wondered how Robert would react when he found out. She was glad she intended to be in his life and help him adjust to anything that upset him.

The first customer arrived about 10:00 A.M. Both Connie and Alice were a little nervous. As suggested by Mei Lin, Connie greeted the lady and introduced herself as the owner. Alice continued with the first lady while Connie was greeting two more women. They sold six dresses and at the end of the day, Connie handed Alice $225.

"What is this?" Alice asked.

"It is your half of today's profits. We are splitting it all from now on."

Alice was expecting her $10 per hour to maybe go to $12 per hour. Today she made $22.50 per hour. Now, there were two "rich-feeling" women working the "Dress for Success" outlet.

Alice had longed for a television for years, ever since her parents were deported. Now she thought, I can afford one if I keep making this kind of money. Robert and I won't need the movies every date.

<h1 style="text-align:center">38</h1>

Robert, Jr. was practicing pool when Pete approached him.

"Your partner James did check out. He was never seen practicing in a pool hall, but he did win some big money in private games."

"Did he have a partner?"

"No mention of a partner. You will be driving to Pittsburgh day after tomorrow: Leave at 5 A.M."

For the first time since he joined the gang two years ago, Robert, Jr. felt reservations. He had cash in his pocket and his only expenses were campground rent and food and, of course, movies. He didn't need the heist money right now and thought how terrible it would be to get caught now that Alice was in his life. No, he said to himself: I'm not going to take any chances right now. If we win a big game, I will quit the gang and live openly. That will make Alice happy, and it feels good to see her smiling. I will call Pete tomorrow and tell him I am sick. One of the other "buds" has a CDL and can drive the truck. I am relieved that I don't have to question James about his life any longer.

James walked into the pool hall and before he could say hello to Robert, Jr., Pete approached him.

"The boys in Chicago told me they know you."

"What boys in Chicago and why were you checking on me?"

"When you told me about your money-laundering scrape with the law, I thought you might be the law. I had to be sure you are not pumping Robert, Jr. for information."

"Pete, I am just playing pool now. I have no other interest in a money-making scheme. Don't tell me anything you are doing; I don't want to know."

"Let me know if you change your mind. I can always use a man who knows his way around."

Robert, Jr. observed them talking and wondered why Pete still had an interest in James. He hoped James wasn't involved in anything illegal. He didn't want to lose his pool partner, and he liked the guy.

"Hi, are we still going to Chicago this weekend?"

"Of course. I bought your flight ticket" and handed it to him." I am going over earlier as I have some business to finish up there."

Robert, Jr. was disappointed they wouldn't be traveling together.

"I will meet you at the hotel about 5: we can have dinner and the game starts at 7. You will need to check your 'stick' on the airplane. They won't let you carry it on. See you Saturday. Keep your eye sharp: the competition will be much better."

James took the train to Newark and got into his BMW at the airport parking lot. He didn't want to make that drive in one day. He would stay over in Pittsburgh. He reached in his trousers' waistband and removed the Derringer. Don't need that pressing in my stomach while I drive, and he put it in the console compartment beside him. During the drive he thought a lot about Evelyn and a little about Connie and Robert, Jr.

39

Freedom Flight

"Jenny, I could use your help with a word. What can I substitute for 'discover'? I have already used that word several times."

"How about 'unearth'?" she responded.

"Yes, I like that."

"How many pages have you written since you started two months ago?"

"Fifty-two. Getting the information is easier than writing about it. I have an idea but have difficulty putting it in words that I like. I find myself re-writing sentences frequently. I wonder if all writers have that problem."

"I would suspect they do. It seems natural to want to express yourself as articulately as possible."

"I never had that problem at the bank. I guess I didn't care as long as my written word was clearly understood. Writing with the readers' reaction in mind is much different. Telling the stories of convicts' lives before and after their prison life, as they have told it to me, comes fairly easy. However, the articulation, as you so accurately described it, is a slower process for me."

"Are you finding it therapeutic, or just hard work?"

"Both! At first, it didn't feel therapeutic; however, as time goes on, I do feel some anger dissipating. I am not the only innocent man who has gone to prison. I used to be consumed with asking myself, why me? I do that far less often now as I realize I am not alone. Many others have suffered the same fate and for much more serious crimes. I never believed other inmates when I heard them say they were innocent of the crime that had them incarcerated. Now at the 'rehab' meetings, many of them do convince me that they were 'just at the wrong place at the wrong time'. Nearly all of them are struggling to find decent paying jobs. I am much more fortunate: I have your support. They don't have anyone, except each other."

"What made you decide to become a banker?'

"I just fell into it. Six months after graduating from DePaul University, the college arranged for my interview on campus. My business degree presented me the opportunity and my personality landed me the job. Following the human resources initial interview, I then met with a bank Vice-President. I recognized immediately that he was a 'high I' type person. My psychology class taught me how to identify an individual's personal decision-making behavior styles. I was able to mirror his style easily, and he decided that he was comfortable with me. If I had not recognized his 'high I', my natural 'high C' might not have pleased him personally. Nevertheless, my natural style is what made me successful at the bank."

"What is a 'high I' and 'high C'?"

"To completely answer that question would require a textbook and two weeks of study. However, 'I' and 'C' are two of the four predominant styles and are direct opposites. An 'I' person will always want to tell you all about themselves. It is easy to get them to be comfortable with you if you seem very interested in their lives and stories, especially if you continue to ask them questions so they can tell you more. A 'C' person likes to analyze everything possible before making a decision. He or she wants all the details, data and facts in order to be prepared to make a decision. You can see why they are opposites. If the 'C' candidate starts talking details, without prioritizing the 'I' preference, the conversation will be mutually unsatisfactory. Often people don't get the jobs for that very reason even though they are well qualified. They never understand why. If the bank VP is a good manager, he will eventually ask for the candidate's verbalization of the details he needs even though that conversation is solicited out of necessity, not out of a preference to bond."

"What are the other two styles?"

"A 'high D' likes to make decisions as soon as possible and move on to the next decision even though they sometimes do not have sufficient details. A 'high S' likes to make friends and trust the other person before making a decision. He or she wants the used car salesperson to be a friend and trustworthy before deciding to buy a car from him or her. As opposed to the 'high D' who doesn't care if the salesperson is worthy of trust. The decision will be made based on the facts he or she considers important regardless of the salesperson's nature."

"That is interesting. What am I?"

"That is why the two-week study period is required. If I answered that question now, there is a high probability that you wouldn't agree with me. Nearly everyone asks that question when first introduced to the subject. It is natural response. The answer is more complex than my simplification. Few people ever see themselves as others see them. The most important thing to take away from this brief introduction is that there isn't any one style preferable to another. Understanding the differences only provides the opportunity to assess and understand a person. It does not provide the assurance of success. You can understand the knowledge and remain unable to utilize it successfully. The first element to master is the acceptance of your own natural style as opposed to your professional style. Secondly, it is not easy to adapt yourself to an opposite style person. It just isn't natural. However, if you are able to master this skill, it opens windows that you couldn't see through previously. Even your personal relationships will blossom and become a greater source of pleasure."

"Jeffrey, will you help me study the textbook?"

"It is the least I can do after all you have done for me."

40

"Do you like watching TV?"

"I don't have one. No phone either. It is becoming harder all the time to find a public phone".

"Robert, do you see the day coming when you will have a cell phone? I would like to be able to call you."

"Yes, I do."

"I am thinking about getting a TV. Your mother is splitting her profits with me now and I can afford it. I was debating what package to get: thought you might help me decide. Are sports of interest to you?"

"Not really, but I do enjoy gangster movies."

"Oh Robert, I hope your interest changes to sports, and you forget the gangster world!"

"Alice, I don't think about gangsters when I am with you."

"Have you moved into your mom's apartment yet?"

"No, I was hoping you would invite me to live here."

"Robert, men and women don't live together after three dates."

"Why not? We have already kissed."

Alice realized he was "dating inept" but this was ridiculous!

"Robert, a kiss is not love, moving in is, or at least it is to me. It takes time to fall in love. You should know something about me. I made a decision as a teenager to not have sex until I was married. I know that isn't typical today, but it is how I feel."

"How long do we have to date to fall in love and get married and live together?"

"For the second time, within seconds, she was alarmed at his naiveté."

"A lot longer than three dates. We need to know each other and understand the needs of each other before we fall in love. For instance, how did you get that scar on your neck?'

"Does it show?"

"No, I felt it when we kissed."

"I don't think it is a scar. I have always had it."

"May I look at it?"

He nodded and she pulled his collar down.

"Robert, it is actually very attractive. Have you ever looked at it in a mirror?"

"No."

"Didn't your mother ever tell you about it?"

"No."

"It looks like a small bird with its wings opened up. I think it is a birth mark and not a scar."

Robert had previously asked her to go clothes shopping with him. James had told him that he needed to wear sports jacket and dress trousers to the pool event. His jeans and pullover T-shirt wouldn't "cut the mustard". Alice was happy to oblige.

The movie Alice had selected was a cowboy story titled "Hostiles". She thought it was a man's movie and the last date they had seen a movie about a woman. When they reached her apartment building after the movie, he asked: "Can I kiss you good night again?"

"I would be very disappointed if you didn't." This kiss was not much improved over the first one. She thought maybe I will need to do some more coaching on our next date.

As Robert walked to the subway, he had a lot to think about. He did want to live with Alice. His only kiss before Alice was in the sixth grade. A group of girls in his class carried mistletoe and attacked the boys they liked. They grabbed the boy's arms and took turns kissing him. When they grabbed him, he struggled free but not before three of them put their lips on his. He found their behavior disgusting. Some other boys did not. They chased after the girl they liked best: grabbed her and got another kiss. The girls seemed to love the game and continued until the Principal heard about it.

Alice's kiss was much different.

41

Freedom Flight

"I met a young woman today who is homeless. She was convicted of child abuse of her four-year-old son and served a one-year sentence."

"What kind of work did she do before being arrested?"

"She was a prostitute since she was fourteen. Her mother was also a prostitute and began 'selling her' as a child. She was raped when she was sixteen and one of those four boys is the father of her now six-year-old son."

"Who is the six-year-old living with?"

"A prostitute friend of her mother took him in."

"Does she get to see him?"

"Yes, she meets him after school."

"Are you going to write about her life in prison in your book?"

"She didn't want to talk about those experiences. I think she is blocking them out."

"Jeffrey, do you think we could help her find a new life with her boy?"

"How could we do that? We can't give her financial aid."

"We could let them live here and let her son experience a loving home. Maybe she would be willing to go to school and get educated in an area that would enable her to get a job. You could invite her here for a meal, and then we could decide. If we do try, we can always abandon the effort if it isn't working. Never having my own child, I have always wished I could help raise a young person. It would be so rewarding."

"I would think just caring for me would be tiring enough."

"Our time isn't tiring, only very satisfying. My life felt empty before you arrived. Now I feel worthwhile just being a part of your life, not withstanding when you physically fill me up with your masculine desire. Could I interest you in some 'one in one' time? My appetite is raging."

"You exhausted me last night. Do you think my boy can be aroused again so soon?"

"Just trying will be pleasurable enough. If he gets interested, it will be a bonus."

She pulled down the zipper and put her hand inside his shorts and squeezed his soft tool. Kneeling on the carpeted living room floor, she pulled the shorts down and slowly engaged her taste buds. She massaged his balls with one hand and stroked his uncircumcised penis with the other. In seconds, she felt his hardness as her tongue licked the 'cone'. It was better than any ice cream she had ever tasted, and she savored every lick.

"Oh, Jenny, that's perfect. Don't change anything. Keep pulling that skin back and forth. It feels so good. I am going to give it to you."

42

The American Airlines ticket to Chicago was first-class. Robert, Jr. did not tell James he had never flown. Waiting in security lines, taking off his shoes, and being frisked were all new and surprising. He didn't even realize his seat was larger and more spacious than most others on the plane. He was glad his seat partner was absorbed with a headset and didn't make any attempt to talk. Sitting idle in luxury, he had time to do nothing but think. Most of his thoughts were about Alice. He wanted to win her over and that meant winning the pool event. He knew his hand would be steady: he had a lot to shoot for.

The hotel room was also luxurious or at least it seemed that way to him. It was only 2 P.M. and James wasn't meeting him until 5:00. The wind was bitter cold: nevertheless, he decided on a walk. The cold had never bothered him too much: he preferred it to the heat and high humidity. The Manhattan concrete in the summer seemed to create a sauna effect, or at least it seemed that way as he had never been in a sauna. He didn't think Chicago looked any different than Manhattan.

He was very concerned when he tried to call James's room and was informed that he didn't have a reservation. At 4:45, James called and said: "Come on down to the lobby and bring your things."

"Aren't we playing pool?"

"Yes, but the plans changed a little."

As they left the hotel, the valet pulled up in the BMW and James said: "Get in, put your bag in the trunk" and then the lid popped open.

"Why don't you have a room? Where are you staying?"

"We will be leaving right after the game finishes. I will explain later."

After dinner in a restaurant that Robert, Jr. had never seen the likes of, they drove to an exclusive neighborhood. The mansion they approached had iron gates. James parked on a side street, and they walked to the gate. Pushing the button James announced himself: "Nine-ball in the corner", and then a car pulled up from the house. A chauffeur got out and opened the back door for them to climb in. Robert, Jr. found it all very mysterious. Why didn't they drive the BMW through the gate? he was thinking. The inside of the house was nearly beyond belief with thick oriental carpets and chandeliers that must have weighed a ton each. They were led through three large doors before they reached the game room. There were five pool tables so far apart that the ball positions were not observable from the adjacent table. James and Robert, Jr. arrived first, and the other teams quickly entered the room. Everyone was wearing a sports coat which they hung neatly on hangers. The long-sleeved shirts were mostly one size larger to provide extra room when moving their arms. Robert, Jr. was easily the youngest person in the room by at least fifteen years. No warm-up time was granted. Promptly at 7 P.M., five "breaks" took place simultaneously. Robert, Jr. was impressed with the organization just as two weeks earlier. Introductions were missing and pleasantries were absent. The $50,000 cash was neatly stacked on a lamp table. Robert, Jr. thought it even looked like big money. The opponents played with intimidating facial expressions. Robert, Jr. thought: I can put on a mean face also, and he did. His competitive adrenalin had never flowed so strongly which only magnified his confidence. He didn't feel any pressure, and it was as if the adrenaline exuded from his fingertips with every shot. He had heard guys talking about being in the "zone" but never had personally experienced it. His confidence level was so high he figured this must be what they were talking about. He knew every makeable shot, and even some unmake able ones were going in. James held up his end, but he thought he played even better. They only lost one game the entire evening and that was James's missed shot. After eleven games and two hours of absolute concentration, the pot was handed to James. He counted $2,500 and gave it to the host. Then, softly he said: "Put this in your pocket and stay close to me."

James moved hurriedly to the clothes rack and grabbed their jackets. Robert, Jr. was in complete confusion. They exited before the only other remaining team. Just before they went into the cold,

James pulled the Derringer from inside his waist band and said: "Follow close."

They ran through some bushes on the side of the house and climbed a six-foot high stone wall. As they approached the car, they were confronted by two men with guns pointed in their direction. James shot first and both fell to the ground. They had not seen the Derringer.

"You drive and I will ride shotgun."

He directed Robert, Jr. to the freeway and they headed east. After an hour of driving, James said: "Pull into this rest area and park where we can see the cars entering."

After parking, Robert, Jr. finally spoke: "How did you know we were going to be robbed?"

"It happened to me once before, and I recognized an opponent tonight that I suspected. I hoped parking on the street would prevent us being followed. Obviously, they were watching when we arrived."

"Is that when you started carrying the Derringer?"

"No, I was already carrying it."

"Did they get the money that time?"

"No, I left two men lying in the street just like tonight. Looks like we have not been followed…park in full view in front of the restaurant. Let's get some coffee."

"I don't drink coffee, but I do need a coke."

They sat by the window and James watched every person entering.

"Robert, Jr., your shot-making tonight was unbelievable! I hope the element of danger doesn't discourage you from continuing to be my partner, but I will certainly understand if it does."

"Not so, I found everything about this trip exciting! I do want to carry a gun to protect myself, though."

"You have proven yourself as a pool player and life-threatening risk taker. Here, take 50% of the money, and we will be full partners. Word travels even in this secretive group of pool 'betters.' You witnessed that Pete was able to learn about me from his Chicago contacts. If you want to continue as my partner, you will need to lower your profile. You can no longer hang out with your "buds" at the pool room, and you must avoid becoming involved with those heist jobs."

"How did you know about that?"

"You don't think I would have invited you into this high-stakes life without knowing everything I could about you? Is your new girl-friend happy with the new store and her new apartment?"

Robert, Jr., after recovering, said: "What else do you know about me?"

"Lots more but now is not the time to discuss that. Let's drive a couple more hours and get rooms for the night. I am pretty sure we are not being followed. We will change cars in Pittsburgh."

Robert, Jr. immediately decided he wouldn't tell Alice about carrying a gun. She wouldn't accept that way of life.

43

Freedom Flight

"Do you know where to find your homeless mother?"

"I think she will be in the park most days. She said she finds it peaceful."

"Bring her home if she is willing; just tell her that I would like to meet her."

"She may resist. Why don't you come to the park with me? She might not trust me without your presence."

"That's true. I should go with you."

As they entered the park, the bright sun was penetrating. The warmth cast a feeling that Jenny relished. Although looking forward to meeting the young woman, she was somewhat ill at ease. It would be a challenge to gain her confidence.

They walked for twenty minutes before Jeffrey spotted her.

"There she is, by the tree looking at the lake."

Jenny observed a pretty woman with a lanky build and long blond hair. Her face looked distraught, and she appeared tired and worn out. Perhaps she wouldn't want to talk.

"Good morning,", Jeffrey offered.

Startled, like out of a trance, the woman made eye contact.

"Oh, hello."

"This is my life-partner, Jenny."

Jenny was now the startled one! She had never heard Jeffrey use that label, and it was reassuring to hear it. Apparently, Jeffrey's feelings for her ran deeper than he had ever verbalized. She wanted to further explore that declaration but now wasn't the time.

"Hello, miss. What is your name?"

"Just call me Missy", the woman responded with reluctance. She obviously wasn't happy about the interruption.

"Jeffrey told me that the two of you had a nice conversation yesterday, and I asked if I could meet you. I am glad we found you so quickly. Do you come here every day?"

The woman apparently was disturbed by Jenny's question.

"I have to go now", and she rapidly started moving toward the lake.

"Please don't go. I would like to be your friend if you will let me."

Missy started running toward the railing that was adjacent to the water. Jeffrey pursued and grabbed her as she was climbing the barrier.

"Don't jump! Life can be better!" he offered.

She began sobbing and her body wilted as she dropped to the ground. Her lifeless form laid there in a state of unconsciousness. Both Jenny and Jeffrey knelt to provide assistance. Wiping the tears from her face, Jenny could see Missy's bruised cheek bone.

"She has been struck, Jeffrey. Pick her up and call 911."

At that moment, she recovered from her unconsciousness and appeared dazed.

"Are you alright?" Jenny asked.

There was no response as Jeffrey lifted her to her feet.

"Can you walk?' Jeffrey asked.

Still no response was forthcoming as she followed Jeffrey's footsteps to a nearby bench. Sitting down, she remained speechless.

"Please call 911. She needs medical attention."

Missy responded by vigorously shaking her head from side to side.

"She doesn't want to go to a hospital, Jenny. Let's take her home. Some bed rest might be all she needs. We can call 911 if she doesn't improve with rest."

44

When they arrived in Manhattan, James called Connie.

"We won the big money in the pool tournament, and Robert, Jr. has agreed to terminate his gang life."

Connie was ecstatic. She rarely displayed excitement, and this was the exception.

"I thought it was going to take months?"

"I did as well but meeting Alice was a bonus I hadn't expected."

"Did he tell you he was dating Alice?"

"No, I saw them going to the movies twice. How do you like the new apartment?"

"Do you see everything we do?"

"Not quite. I do look forward to being able to celebrate all the changes as a family in the not too distant future."

"When do you plan to tell Robert, Jr. that you are his father?"

"I guess that means you are OK with it?'

"Yes."

"He is not ready for anymore new developments just yet, especially about his father. If his relationship with Alice continues to develop, a grandchild may come into the picture. He needs to mature considerably in order to be a good father. I hope to act as his mentor, not father, during his maturation. Oh, and don't be concerned about Evelyn, I do have really strong feelings for her."

Shocked, Connie asked: "You know we are friends?"

"Of course! You don't think I bought that line about 'now he is all yours', do you? I saw the two of you visiting each other's apartments a few times. Remember, I told you I wanted to know about your life before I approached you. I needed to know who your friends were. You don't have many. Is the Chinese woman a good landlord?"

All this new information was too much for Connie to absorb at one time. She felt like her life was a public spectacle. She also felt like James was a trained spy. Then she remembered he said he was an FBI undercover agent but that was twenty-two years ago. The relief was reassuring as she thought: Evelyn is in good arms.

"Are you going to tell Evelyn that you know we are friends?"

"I would rather you did if that is alright with you. After all, you introduced us, and she may harbor some concerns about us."

"I will."

When she hung up the phone, without even thinking, she called Evelyn at the salon and said: "I need to talk to you."

"Is anything wrong?"

"No, I guess everything is right."

As Connie entered Evelyn's apartment, she announced: "Our detective plan didn't work too well. We were detected."

"You mean James knows we are friends?"

"That's right, and Robert, Jr. told him he is quitting the gang life."

"How did that happen so soon?"

"Alice and pool-playing money motivated him. James also knows Mei Lin is our landlord. Given that he knows both our bodies, I am not sure there is anything he doesn't know about us."

"Does he know Mei Lin?"

"He didn't say but I wouldn't be surprised. He seems to be directing all the changes in both our lives. Beyond being in shock, I guess I shouldn't have any complaints. When are you going to see him again?"

"Wednesday. We are having dinner."

"Tell him I expressed thanks for helping Robert, Jr. You take flight, girl."

Evelyn was thinking of Connie's well wishes when she met James at Georgio's. They kissed passionately before they sat down.

"Congratulations on your success with Robert, Jr.! Connie couldn't be happier and asked me to thank you. Even though it was in the distant past, I was very concerned that your shared love might create a problem for her and me."

"Twenty-two years is a long time to hold onto love. Has Connie dated much?"

"Only two or three times and not in the past four years. She says she has given up on men."

"Sounds like we have another restoration to address."

Not that Evelyn expected it would, the love-making and ensuing ecstasy didn't diminish. Each time James pushed with his strong legs, she arched her back responsively and ached for more. She always got more until she totally released her desire.

45

Freedom Flight

"Missy, are you feeling better after your rest? You have been sleeping for twelve hours! You must be hungry. Would you like some ham and eggs?

"Thank you. Yes, I am hungry. It was very kind of you to bring me to your home. I didn't want to be confined in a hospital again."

Jenny was shocked by Missy's vocabulary. She had only spoken a few words before going to bed, and her demeanor now was very changed.

"Missy, do you still want me to call you by that name?"

"You can call me Joan. That is the name my mother gave me. It has been a long time since I have heard it. As Jeffrey no doubt told you, my lifestyle precluded using my birth name."

"Joan, you have a very good vocabulary. Where did you get that education?"

"I have always been a veracious reader. Books revealing the character values of famous people have always interested me. I started reading them when I was eight years old. My teacher recognized my interest and provided the books as a loan. Sometimes I finished a book in one night and returned it the next day."

"You must read very rapidly?"

"My teacher told me that I can read faster than anyone else he had ever taught."

"Do you remember most of what you read?"

"Everything since I was eight. I see it in my mind."

"That is a superb gift. You could use it to your financial advantage. Did you ever consider going back to school to study for a career?"

"I never liked school. The other students knew my mother's livelihood and constantly threw it in my face."

"Did you make good grades in school?"

"No, I didn't study or do homework. I just read biographies."

"What is your son's name?"

"Joseph."

"Joan, I would like to make you a proposal. You can stay here with Jeffrey and me while you put your life together. Eventually, I would like you to bring Joseph here, as well. I never had children, nor did Jeffrey. Perhaps we could act as foster grandparents if he likes us. If it doesn't 'pan out', you have no obligation to continue the arrangement.

"Wow! That is quite a proposal. There is no reason to not accept. I will do what I can to make my presence a benefit to your lives. However, you must assure me that you will ask me to leave if it doesn't 'pan out'."

"We have an agreement. I am anxious to tell Jeffrey."

46

Freedom Flight

"How was your visit with Joseph?"

"He is still distant. He doesn't want to talk to me much about anything. I think he likes going to school but I am not even sure about that. The other kids don't seem to be interested in becoming friends. When he comes out of the school building, they are talking in groups and Joseph is not included. That really bothers me."

"Do you think you will be able to bring him here soon to meet us?"

"The judge said after four months he will review my request to spend more time with him and take him places with me. I can understand the Judge's reluctance based on my lack of good parenting. I was 'in a fog' mentally with my lifestyle, and my mother's influence certainly didn't help. Between her 'Johns' and mine, Joseph was totally alone and confused. The rehab counselor in prison opened my eyes to the damage I was creating. Now it seems impossible that I could have been so blind. Thank goodness I have a second chance. When I first met you, Jenny, I did intend to jump in that lake and end my suffering. I had relapsed the night before and entertained a few of my mother's 'Johns''. I should never have gone to her house to visit. The counselor had warned me not to revisit that scene. However, I wanted to prove to myself and show her that I had put that life behind me. Now I know I haven't. Just as the counselor warned, it is my addiction to feel worthy. When a man gets pleasure from my body, I feel good. It is a 'high'."

"Joan, do you think when you receive Joseph's love and attention it might become a new 'high'? I have been taught that we all need a 'high' in our life on a regular basis. I didn't feel a 'high' until Jeffrey came into my life, and now I feel it every day. Giving and receiving love can be, and is for me, very powerful. Without that 'high', I can easily understand why individuals turn to artificial 'highs' like drugs, alcohol and sex. It is my understanding that some people find their 'high' at an early age and live a less stressful life because of it. Children quite often find music, art, or sports to feel 'high'. They are the lucky ones. I hope you find your new 'high' in Joseph, and I will do everything I can to help. I know Jeffrey wants to help as well. He also, without realizing it, is searching for a new 'high'. His career was his only priority and that is gone forever. I don't see any signs that his writing is going to become his new 'pleasure-place'. He struggles with it, but it keeps him busy. When he is pursuing completing his book, he isn't focused on his loss.

47

Robert knew it would not be wise to tell Alice about the shooting. He was an accomplice and the possibility of being identified was very concerning.

When he arrived at her apartment, she said: "I am cooking. I hope you like chicken. I would have called you to ask if you had a phone number."

Robert guessed he would need to remedy that. The thought of answering a phone was unnerving. He preferred his privacy except for Alice, and it would be a bonus to be able to call his mother at any time.

Alice was pleased to hear he had won the pool tournament and wanted to ask how much he won. However, she thought better of it. She was glad to hear that he was moving into his mother's apartment so at least now they would know where he was sleeping.

They both enjoyed the chicken and Alice's new television. He found the "Guide" button fascinating and finally she asked: "Can we watch a program now and stop playing the 'Guide'?"

He felt a bit embarrassed and they settled on a detective program.

Before leaving, he blurted out: "I am not going to hang-out with the 'buds' anymore. James said it was not a good idea now that I am playing big-money games."

"That's wonderful. I would like to meet this James and personally thank him."

"Sure, he seems like a nice guy. Maybe we can have lunch someday."

As he said, "nice guy", he was startled by himself. Does a "nice guy" shoot two people and drive off? Robert did find James to be a mystery. His Chicago background, knowing where to find the big-money games and carrying a Derringer were not typical behaviors. On a personal level, he seemed to offer good counsel and to be sincere. Robert wasn't accustomed to that kind of friendship. Introducing him to Alice would be an interesting experience.

48

James was very concerned that Robert, Jr. was a party to the shooting. Following the shooting and immediately after parting with him at the motel in Pittsburgh, he phoned the Police Department to tell them what had occurred. They revealed that both men were reported to be in fair condition and were wanted for previous criminal activity. He would need to come to the Chicago PD to complete the paperwork for the incident. No mention of his pool partner would be on the record. The fact that Robert, Jr. was aware of his readiness to defend himself was also very concerning. He needed to remedy that, and the only way he could think of to fix the situation was to level with Robert, Jr. about his Police connection. They had arranged to meet in two days for breakfast after arriving back in Manhattan.

"I was thinking you might be reluctant to meet with me after what happened in Chicago. I apologize for getting you involved in that fracas. I thought we could get out of town without being attacked by parking the car on the side street. If I had expected a shooting, I would not have taken you with me."

"James, I am confused about you."

"I am sure you are. Let's just say I have law enforcement connections. The two men I shot are going to recover and are wanted as criminals. The police know I shot them in self-defense, and they don't know and won't know that you were with me. There will not be any investigation."

"Do you shoot people often?"

"It does occur from time to time but only if I have to defend myself. Fortunately, I have never killed anyone. My aim is pretty good, and I practice at the range three times a week. I don't want you carrying a gun because you are not trained. If you ever decide you want law enforcement training, I can arrange it for you."

"Are we still going to play pool for money?"

"Of course. I like the money, and hopefully you will not witness any more shootings."

Robert, Jr. was relieved knowing that James was not being pursued for the shootings. His discomfort diminished when he realized the incident would not affect his relationship with Alice. Already he knew she was the best thing that ever happened in his life.

"James, I have a girlfriend who would like to meet you. I really like her and don't want to disappoint her. Would you have lunch with us?"

"Certainly, I am pleased you have someone. I am sure you didn't tell her about the shooting, correct?"

"No, I wouldn't want her to be involved."

"Good, I knew I could trust you to use good judgment. Thursday for lunch is good on my schedule."

"I will check her schedule.

49

James called: "We have a situation we need to discuss but it's nothing to worry about. Can we have dinner tonight?"

"Yes, just tell me where and what time?"

James arrived early and sat in an inconspicuous booth. Fifteen minutes later, Connie walked in on time.

"Is my son having second thoughts about quitting the gang life?"

"No, he seems to be firm on that. It's just that he wants me to meet Alice. She asked him to introduce us since I influenced him to quit the gang. She wants to thank me personally, and I know she saw me in the store. I can't tell him I won't meet her as it might be a set-back on the relationship I have with him. You either need to assure her secrecy or I need to tell Robert, Jr. who I am, and I think it is too early to do that. Can you trust her to keep the secret from him? Is she trustworthy?"

"Yes, but I think you need to tell her yourself because I have told her that you are a friend of Robert Young, and I don't want to be the one confessing my lie. I think she really likes Robert, Jr., and I don't want to do anything that will harm that relationship."

"I will do the best I can, and I think you should be with me when I tell her. We need to do it tomorrow because I am having lunch with her and Robert, Jr. on Thursday."

Connie invited Alice for dinner to celebrate the store's success. Just before they sat down to dine on pulled pork, a knock on the apartment door was heard.

"Hello, James. I will set a plate for you."

"Hi Connie, and you must be Alice?"

"Hello, I saw you in the old store one day."

"That's right, you did."

"Connie told me you are an old friend of Robert, Jr.'s father."

"Yes, I asked her to do that, but it wasn't the truth. The 'fib' wasn't hers but mine. I did it to protect Robert, Jr. from the truth."

"Is he in trouble?"

"No, I am the trouble: I am, or was, Robert Young. I am Robert, Jr.'s father."

He proceeded to tell the story taking the blame as he had when he gave Connie the cashier's check.

"Connie, no wonder you were in shock after he left the store. I knew something wasn't right."

"I am asking you to keep this secret from Robert, Jr. until I think the time is right for him to know."

"If that will keep him off the streets, I absolutely will. How long do you think it will take before you tell him?"

"I really have no idea how our friendship will develop. I do believe he trusts me now, but he needs to open-up to me before I will risk telling him, and I want Connie with me when I do. Alice, you can help speed up the process by occasionally asking him about me. Your feed-back will let me know how he is feeling about me."

"Of course, I can do that. We are still having lunch tomorrow, right?"

"As scheduled", James replied. "I have asked Mei Lin to join us for dinner, Connie, if that is alright?"

In total surprise, Alice asked: "You know Mei Lin?"

"Yes, she is my father's sister"

"Oh my, now I know why I have this free apartment. Robert Jr.'s family is going to grow quickly when he finds out."

Connie was also just learning that Mei Lin was James's aunt. Her good fortune could have arrived in a cookie, she thought. As they dined, Mei Lin and James described their lives in China. While picking up the dirty dishes, Alice asked: "James, may I see the birthmark on your neck?"

Connie felt uneasy as she heard James answer: "Yes."

"Oh my, it is exactly like Robert, Jr.'s. That is so remarkable."

"Even more remarkable is that my father had the same mark, also. I didn't know Robert Jr. had the birthmark. I will need to be sure he doesn't see mine. I guess it is in the 'DNA'. It is even more ironic that both my father and I flew to China to escape, and now Robert, Jr. is flying to Alice to escape the gang life. The bird with expanded wings has flown all three of us to safety."

Everyone was silent for a moment as they considered the irony or was it the universe protecting the family? Mei Lin spoke first: "Good fortune follow good people. The flying bird drops seeds to someday harvest."

The other three just looked at each other while digesting the words of prophecy. Alice wondered for the first time if that bird would eventually seed her. The thought of the possibility made Alice weak in the knees.

James bid everyone good night and walked down the stairs to the street. Feeling very good about the family conversation, he decided to stop on the way to feed his pigeons.

50

Freedom Flight

"Joseph, these are my friends – Jenny and Jeffrey. I live here now, and they are helping me to be a better person. I don't have all those 'uncles' visiting me now. They want to be your friend, also."

Joseph was silent as he fidgeted with his hands in his pockets. Jenny thought he was interested in getting to know them although the thought was, no doubt, based strictly on hope.

"Joseph, would you like to see the room where your mom sleeps?"

When Joseph did not respond, Jenny took his hand which was surrendered without reluctance.

"She has two beds, and you can sleep in one if you ever visit us."

Joseph immediately went to a bed and tried the mattress comfort. It was apparent he wasn't in any hurry to stand-up,

"Joseph, your mom wants you to come and stay with us one night. Would you like that?"

Instantly, he nodded his head in the affirmative.

"When you come maybe we can go fishing in the park. Do you like fishing?" Jeffrey asked, all the while knowing it was very unlikely, he had ever held a fishing pole, or had even seen one. He made the offer out of impulse and then realized he hadn't thought about fishing since leaving prison. It had always been his favorite pastime.

"Do you have a pole?"

It was Joseph's first words since meeting his new friends.

"Jeffrey, why don't you and Joseph walk down to the hardware store and get new fishing gear and a license?"

Jenny's suggestion was welcomed by Jeffrey since he had painted himself into a corner with his impulsive offer.

"Great idea! Let's go Joseph."

Without hesitation, Joseph bolted towards the door.

"Jenny, I would like to have the social worker visit your home if that is OK? She must approve any location where Joseph resides. I am sure she will be glad to remove him from his current residence. Although his caretaker is a responsible woman and doesn't have any of her 'Johns" visit her house, I believe the social worker suspects her profession. Social services didn't have any space in a foster home when they took him from me."

"Joan, have you given any more thought about going back to school and what you might want to study?"

"Yes, my parole officer has arranged for me to attend a trade school starting next month. I will receive free tuition as a rehab student."

"That is great! I didn't know educational rehab programs existed. What are you going to study?"

"I would like to be creative and welding sparks my interest."

"Welding?! That is a surprise given your photographic memory skill."

"I know but academic subjects just don't interest me. I can learn easily by reading about most anything, but it is using my hands and creative instincts that I want to pursue. Welding sculptures that I designed would be very uplifting for me, I think."

"That is intriguing, and I am excited for you! How long would it take to complete the course?"

"If I pass all the examinations every quarter, one year is the minimum. If I fail an exam, I can retake it only once to maintain my tuition-free program."

"It is wonderful that our government has finally taken positive action to help convicts improve their lives. Could you work as an industrial welder as well?"

"Oh, yes, I would receive certification. Good welders make a good wage, and I could support Joseph's needs without any difficulty. We could have our own place, and I could hire a babysitter when he is home from school, and I am still working."

"Joan, I would love to baby sit Joseph, and he could ride the school bus from here. I think he and Jeffrey are going to be good for each other. Perhaps the universe is providing direction for all of us. Let's not miss the opportunity that has been given us."

"You're so right, Jenny. I hadn't recognized it yet, but you are so right. I feel blessed for the first time in my life. What a great feeling."

51

Freedom Flight

"Look at those poles! They can probably catch really big fish," Jenny announced when Jeffrey and Joseph came through the front door.

"Look mom, we have hooks to catch the fish. We put worms on them, and the fish want to eat the worms."

"Where did you learn that Joseph?" his mom asked.

"Jeffrey told me all about fishing. We are going today."

Joan was beside herself. She had never seen Joseph look so happy and excited. Her son was actually acting normal. The realization was overwhelming. Her joy was unbridled. She thought: if this is the 'high' Jenny talked about, she was certainly accurate. This feeling surpasses my wildest dreams. I didn't know it was possible. I will remember and treasure this very moment forever regardless of any negative circumstances that might occur. I know this memory and feeling will prevail. I want to see that joy on his face as often as possible.

"When can we go?"

"Let's have some lunch and plan our outing while we eat", Jeffrey responded.

During lunch, Joseph opened-up like a can of sweet peaches. He was non-stop talk and rambled about everything that came to his mind. He didn't ask any questions and seemed only to need to verbally express himself. Mostly he told stories about the other kids in kindergarten. He expressed deep interest in how different their lives were from his own.

"Karen sits beside me and talks all the time, but I never talk to her. She has a dog named Fluffy, and they sleep together. She takes him for a walk in her yard every morning except when it is raining. Then her mother takes him. Her dad has already gone to work as a policeman."

"Joseph, does Karen ever ask you any questions about your life?" Jenny asked.

"Sometimes."

"What do you tell her?"

"I just don't answer."

"Could you tell her that you went fishing with your new friend Jeffrey?"

"Maybe I could. I'll see."

"She probably really wants to know you since she tells you so much about her life. Maybe she really needs a friend."

"Maybe."

"Joseph, if you have finished your lunch, you should probably go to the bathroom before we catch that big fish." Jeffrey offered.

Joseph's pole was twice his height. Apparently, the store didn't have any kids' poles. As they went out the door, Joseph's pole got caught in the door frame. Jeffrey quickly remedied the situation, and down the porch steps Joseph ran with his pole leading the way and causing him to stumble without harm. He raised himself, looked quizzically at his pole and continued on his way without any show of concern.

"Jenny, I can't thank you enough for providing the environment and the friendship to 'free' Joseph from himself."

"He certainly did an immediate one-eighty, didn't he? His emotions were apparently 'bottling' up his need to express himself: A small amount of attention to his personal interests was all he needed to release his emotions. He appears to be smart. Has the school tested his intelligence?"

"If they have, they haven't told me, and that is understandable given my circumstances. I have often wondered if he has a memory like mine."

52

Lunch the following day went pretty much as expected. Alice asked James about his life, and his responses were consistent with what he had already told Connie and Robert, Jr. James in turn asked Alice about her life and Robert, Jr. learned a few things he had never asked her. Since the store profits continued to grow, she was now sending some money to her parents in the Philippines. The used-clothing market was obviously strong, and word of mouth was spreading. A half dozen new customers were coming in every day. Not everyone purchased but most did. Mei Lin promoted the new business at every opportunity. The relationship between the three continued to become closer now that Connie knew Mei Lin was Robert, Jr.'s great aunt. In addition, Mei Lin's gracious and delicious dinners were a distinct change from everyday menus.

Connie called Evelyn and brought her up to date on the secret agreement with Alice. Both shared their positive feelings about the development. Evelyn revealed that she and James were planning a weekend in Philadelphia. She wasn't a history buff but going any-where with him was fine by her.

Alice now had a strong motivation to assist with James's plan. He appeared to be a good role model for Robert which is something he had never had. It was a surprise when she received a phone call from Robert. It was from a new number and not one from a phone booth.

"Did you buy a phone?"

"Yes, but I don't know how to use it. Can I come over tonight so you can teach me?"

"I think I can do that", was her answer.

When he arrived, she could see his excitement.

"This thing is quite complicated", he muttered.

Alice was well aware by now that Robert's self-induced isolation made him appear to be of limited intelligence. She didn't believe that to be the case and had made it her personal challenge to prove it wasn't.

"When you learn to use it, you will really like it. We will go slowly as you can't learn it all at once. I think we should start with a hello kiss."

She put her hands on his face and pulled him close. She had decided this was going to be a passionate kiss. He puckered up his tight lips and touched hers without any feeling.

"Robert, soften your lips and let them be a little moist. Now, let's try that again."

She gave him a long moist kiss with her tongue touching his. He felt his body react to her kiss and momentarily lost his self-awareness. He was only aware of the feeling she was giving him.

"Can we do that again?" he asked.

"Certainly, when we are alone you can kiss me as often as you like. Just remember, only kissing, nothing more."

They kissed again, and quickly he learned to explore inside her mouth with his tongue, just as she was doing to him. Now he was fully aware that his penis was very hard. Just like it was when he woke-up most mornings. He wanted to put it in his hand but instinctively knew he couldn't do that. Alice felt his reaction against her thigh and said: "It's OK; you don't have to hide your feelings. Just be relaxed and don't be concerned. Your body is just being masculine, and I am not embarrassed by your natural reaction." As soon as he relaxed, his penis exploded with pleasure and Alice was well aware.

"Are you more relaxed now?"

He didn't answer, only smiled.

"Let's sit down and look at your new phone."

He was only able to concentrate on the phone for about ten minutes, and then he started kissing her again. He didn't learn much about the phone, but his boxer shorts got very wet. She was pleased to be the first woman in his life to have given him that experience. It did surprise her that he could have multiple orgasms with his penis remaining in his pants. She had never seen a man's penis, only pictures, and was curious how she would react when she saw his. She hoped that would happen sooner rather than later. If they were ever to get married, she didn't want it to be that Robert only wanted an orgasm. He could have one as often as he liked: no pressure to get married. Feeling him having orgasms did excite her and accelerate her desire to do the same. She thought maybe I am the one who will feel pressure to get married. I do hope that our relationship continues to build quickly. Robert's company is very enjoyable, and I can see myself falling in love. She felt that guiding him to maturity suited her well.

53

Freedom Flight

"Mom, look at my fish! I caught it on my second try. Jeffrey didn't get his until his third try."

"What kind of fish is it, son?"

"It is a carp, mom. Have you ever seen one before?"

"I don't think I have."

"Jeffrey says we can't eat it because it doesn't taste good. He threw his back in, but I wanted to show you mine."

"It is really a nice one, Joseph. Do you want to go fishing again?"

"Sure do, and I can tell Karen about fishing."

"That is nice. I am sure she will want to hear your story."

"Can we stay here tonight, Mom? I would like to go fishing again tomorrow. Maybe you can come too, and I can show you how to do it."

"That is a great idea if Jenny and Jeffrey are OK with it. Remember, this is their house, and we are invited guests. We don't want to be unkind and overstay our welcome."

"Is it OK if we stay?"

"Certainly, let's do a one-night try and see how it goes. Maybe you will not like your bed and won't be able to sleep." Jenny responded.

"Oh, I am sure I will sleep."

"Joseph, please thank Jenny for her offer."

"Thank you."

Once in bed, and seemingly very comfortable, Joseph volunteered: "Mom, I sure like your new friends."

"I am glad. You should give thanks for our good luck to have met them."

After tucking her son in, Joan walked back to the kitchen.

"Joan, has social services given you permission to permit Joseph to live here?"

"I should hear from them this week. I am quite confident they will approve despite Jeffrey's parole status. How is he progressing with his book? He hasn't asked me; however, I would be glad to tell him about my prostitute life before prison. Maybe some young woman may read it and will benefit from reading about my circumstances. I would love to help someone who is suffering from desperation just as you must feel by rescuing me."

"That would be a wonderful addition to his writing. I will tell him about your offer and facilitate the conversation if that would make him more comfortable. He might be uneasy asking you some questions."

"That is fine. I will tell him any detail that you or he feel will be a contribution to his work. Perhaps my experiences will further motivate his writing. I can sense his need to find satisfaction with himself once again. Being falsely convicted and seen as a criminal by the entire world must be devastating to his self-esteem."

54

Riding the subway home, Robert, Jr. began to feel a little guilty. He had felt a multitude of sexual satisfaction, and Alice felt none: that didn't seem fair. He needed to talk to her about that. There was no doubt in his mind that he was ready to marry her right now and wondered how long it would take her to feel the same way.

James had arranged another pool event in Philadelphia for the weekend. It had only been two weeks since their last event, and he had been practicing at various pool halls across town on a regular basis. They met at their usual lunch spot and discussed the plan for the weekend. James was traveling early again and had made a plane reservation for Robert, Jr. James's announced that he intended to bring Evelyn. His mother had told him they were dating. They were staying at a different hotel, and James explained the arrangement was to protect their partnership from being detected prior to the big money game. He further explained that they could not win every event, or they would eventually be "black-balled". James's plan was to win no more than two out of every three events. His plan this Saturday was to lose the final "ladder game". Therefore, he would be paying all expenses for Robert, Jr. The plan to lose intentionally did not sit well with Robert, Jr.; however, he trusted James's judgment. Were it not for James, he would still be taking part in house burglaries.

"James, since you are taking Evelyn, I would like to take Alice."

"That's fine but we cannot socialize as couples during the weekend. The girls could meet inconspicuously for dinner Saturday night if they wish while we are playing pool. Since we will not be carrying any winnings after the game, it will be safe for us to use separate cabs for the event. I will call you on Saturday at 5 P.M. to give you the address."

Robert, Jr. called Alice immediately after the lunch and invited her to fly with him on Friday. She reacted with excitement and asked: "Can we see the Liberty Bell and the Mint?"

"We can see whatever you like."

She thought his willingness to expand his comfort zone was encouraging.

"Robert, I will need to ask your mother for time-off from the store, but I don't expect it will be a problem. She seems to like the idea that we are dating. Just one thing, Robert, we will need two rooms. Can you afford that?"

"Why two rooms? I will always respect your decision to remain a virgin until we are married."

"Robert, I am happy you are planning on our marriage. However, I don't trust myself to lie in bed beside you and not want our physical intimacy. Just because I am not enjoying sex with you doesn't mean I don't want to. When we kissed endlessly the other night, my body was aching for you. Giving you sexual satisfaction was my only relief from my own desires. Women do have the same urges as men."

"Why don't we get married then? How do you know when you are in love?"

"When being with the other person is your first priority: when you would rather be with that person more than anything else in life."

"Then I am definitely in love. How about you?"

"Every day I feel more that way. Let's see how the weekend together feels."

Robert hung up the phone with additional hope for their marriage and all the added benefits such as not needing two rooms. The pace of his heartbeat increased at the thought of laying his nude body against hers all night long. It sounded to him like this weekend could determine Alice's final decision.

Alice hung up the phone and was surprised by her own words to Robert. She guessed she was more comfortable with the thought of marrying Robert, sooner rather than later. He was not hesitant to change his behavior at her beckoning. She did feel she could make him happy as a husband, and his willingness to please her made her life more complete. Her words in response to his questions unveiled deeper feelings than she had recognized. Being with him for three consecutive days would be important, and there were some things she still needed to discuss with him."

55

Freedom Flight

"How was your first welding class? Were you disappointed with anything?"

"It was just an orientation. We really didn't do anything. The instructor just told us what to expect. He did say: 'Some of you have probably already welded, and if you have, I want you to forget everything you learned. It will only impede your progress to do it correctly. There are many poor welders trying to make a living. When you pass this course, you will be an excellent welder. I don't certify welders who are less than excellent. I have a reputation to maintain and liabilities to protect. If you graduate from this class and do less than expert welding and contribute to someone's death, it could be traced back to me. If that scares you then you should leave this room now. This is a serious responsibility you are embarking upon.' I had never considered that possibility and it does foster some serious thought. Even though my goal is to do artwork, I will undoubtedly do industrial work to provide an income. His message resounded with me."

"Did anyone walk out of the classroom?"

"No, but I observed some concern on a couple of faces. When we were walking out of class, a man approached me and asked if I was concerned by the liability comment. I told him no, but I don't think that was his actual motive. Once he received a non-defensive response, he continued a conversation that was more social in nature. He asked me to have coffee with him and I did."

"Well then, tell me about him. Was he charming and good looking?"

"Very! He is a large-boned man with a bulging chest and stands about 6 foot 2. He has a mustache and looks like a welder. He told me I didn't look like any welder he had ever seen. I asked him if that was a compliment, and he said he wouldn't be having coffee with me if it were not. He definitely is a 'player' but a nice one. He is probably 40 years old and, no doubt has plenty of experience with women."

"Is he married or ever been married?"

"I didn't ask him, and he didn't volunteer that information which probably means he is married."

"Are you interested in dating him if he asks?"

"No, I have no interest in dating: way too many bad memories being with men. I only want to concentrate on being a good mother to Joseph and earning an honest living. I will enjoy his conversation though if he continues to pursue me. When he finds out that I am not going to bed with him, I am sure the pursuit will end abruptly, and he will move on to someone else. It won't be with anyone in our class though because I am the only woman with twenty-two men."

56

Freedom Flight

"Jeffrey, Joan met a man in welding class who is interested in her. She says she has no interest in dating. Her prostitute memories are too vivid and negative. I hope someday she can put those memories in a casket and enjoy a male relationship. She has no idea how rewarding that could be. You have completed my life. I was always living with a longing to belong to a man. I think my terrible relationship with my father left a hole in me that needed to be filled up. I want you to know how much I appreciate you."

"Jenny, I am certain your appreciation is miniscule compared to mine. Where would I be today without you? No doubt on the streets like the people I am interviewing. I am more than appreciative: I have become emotionally connected. It gives me joy to see you smile and be happy. I never felt that way before being with you. In fact, all this talk about emotion makes me horny. I am as stiff as a young oak tree and want my oak tree to give you another smile."

"I want your oak tree in me, Jeffrey", and she pulled down his zipper and out sprung his oak tree. She wrapped her fingers around it and stroked the foreskin back and forth vigorously. He reached under her skirt and ripped her panties with his strong hands. Then turning her around and leading her to the back of a kitchen chair. She bent over the chair and he plunged his masculinity through the hole in her panties and into her wet valley. She felt his stiffness immediately and uttered a low groan of pleasure. He was like an animal and thrust back and forth with all the speed he could muster. She had to hold the chair to prevent losing balance as he was pushing her violently.

"Yes baby, you are going to get it all. Take my cock. You like it, don't you?"

His words were very stimulating, and her vagina was erupting. She came with a scream and he came with "Oh, yeah!" They both remained silent for moments and remained bent over the chair and still physically engaged. As he slowly removed his limp penis from her soaked and satisfied femininity, she impulsively said: "Oh, Jeffrey, I loved your dirty talk. That was the biggest and best orgasm you have given me."

She turned around and asked him to sit on the kitchen table. She wrapped her fingers around his exhausted penis and said: "I want it again" as she put his wetness into her mouth.

"Get him hard, baby, and you can have him as often as you want."

Immediately her nipples turned from jelly to granite. She was eagerly anticipating another orgasm or two.

57

Evelyn hailed a cab early Friday morning bound for the airport. She would meet James at the hotel as he had driven down the day prior to conduct some business. At the boarding gate, she was surprised to see Alice and Robert, Jr. They exchanged pleasantries while waiting to board and the women arranged to meet for dinner the next evening.

After checking into the hotel, Alice and Robert became tourists. They climbed aboard a tour bus and viewed all the historic sights while listening as the driver described the locations' significances. Alice was delighted to witness Robert's interest.

"I never liked reading history books in school but seeing it is different."

"Robert, did you ever think about finishing high school? You can't play pool forever to earn a living, and you need to graduate to get a decent job."

"I wasn't very good at studying and making passing grades at school. I don't know if I could graduate."

"I think you could, and I can help you study and learn."

The possibility had never occurred to him but now it had some appeal. None of his "buds" had graduated. It didn't seem necessary before but now it was important to Alice.

"I can try it, nothing to lose, I guess. If I can't make it, can we still get married?"

"Graduating is not a requirement for my love: only that you give it a chance."

"OK, but you will need to tell me how to get started."

"Robert, does James have a high school diploma?"

"I don't know. I never asked him."

"Do you consider him a friend or just a pool partner?"

"I think I would like him to be a friend. He seems to like me and trusts me."

"Good friends share their personal thoughts and opinions. Perhaps you should start a conversation with him about his life. Ask his opinion on something. If he wants to be your friend, he will be glad you asked. If he asks you questions, you should open up to him and be honest. You both need to trust each other with your innermost questions about life to be good friends: just as we are doing in our relationship. I need you to feel comfortable telling me anything without fearing that I will use it to hurt you."

"I do feel that way."

"Someday, when you are ready, I would like you to tell me about your life living on the streets and your gang involvement: not now, just some day."

He didn't answer her: he wasn't ready to confess to be a burglar.

"You know, we would not be dating if James had not arranged for our store to move."

Robert jerked his head sideways and replied with serious concern: "What? James did that?! Why?"

Mei Lin, our landlord and partner in business, is his aunt. He recognized her need to fill the open space and thought your mom's business would be a good fit. He is a good businessman and now his aunt has more income."

"How did you find that out?"

"Mei Lin told us."

Robert initially felt considerable discomfort that James was becoming too involved in their lives. The more he thought about it, the less uncomfortable he became. James was only doing a good thing for everyone. He didn't know that he would be helping with the move or that he would find Alice attractive. He decided it was just meant to be, and he was very glad it did. He was relieved when he concluded that his meeting Alice was not a set-up; he had accomplished that on his own. Then he wondered if James knew that Connie was his mother.

Alice had not intended to tell Robert about James and Mei Lin's family relationship. It just flowed from her lips naturally like it was coming from somewhere else. She felt like Robert was supposed to be told, and she was only the transportation. She didn't feel any discomfort and wondered why. After all, he did need to know at some point that his own family cared about his wellbeing. She hoped that would happen soon: she didn't like having secrets from Robert, but she had agreed to it.

58

Evelyn and James went directly to bed when they met-up in the hotel. Both had pent-up lust and the passion was mutual. It was total lovemaking, not just sex. His pleasure was her pleasure and vice-versa. His oral sex on her felt divine for both of them. Her oral sex on him was foreplay, a prelude to physical intimacy.

In the afternoon, he asked her to take a ride in the car.

"Where are we going, sightseeing?"

"No, I want to look at some property."

"Why would you look for property in Philadelphia?"

"Evelyn, I am not just a pool player, I have other business interests and income."

He seemed to stop there without providing any details.

"I don't need to know anymore; I don't care what you do as long as we can be together as often as possible."

She did wonder why he didn't want to tell her more but was truthful when she said it made no difference. The property they entered was a mansion, Evelyn thought. He looked closely at the paintings and adornments as the realtor said it was being sold furnished. James asked if the asking price was firm, and the answer was no. When he asked why it was being sold, the answer was vague and obviously less than forthright. Evelyn found all of this curious and wondered if James and she would ever live there. She also thought that his businesses must be very successful.

Friday night they went to the theater, not a movie: rather a musical stage play. Evelyn felt embarrassed by her dress as she had never attended such an affair. She shared her feelings with James, and he replied: "Let's buy you an evening dress tomorrow."

She immediately responded: "I didn't mean that."

"I know. I would just like to spoil you a little."

She already felt spoiled in the bedroom every time she took flight: a new dress would be too much. A rich guy who was generous: she guessed if they ever lived together it wouldn't be in her small apartment on Ninth Street.

The shopping spree on Saturday turned out to be more than one dress. He bought her three outfits, shoes and jewelry and said: "Now we won't have to go shopping for a while."

She thought her life had become surreal. He had always worn jeans on their previous dates. This weekend he had brought an expensive suit and sports jacket.

Promptly at 5 P.M., he phoned Robert, Jr. to give him the address.

"I will meet you in the lobby of the house at 6:50."

Alice and Evelyn agreed to meet at Evelyn's hotel at 6. James had made their dinner reservation and put them in a cab. Before he did, Alice said: "James, I told Robert, Jr. that Mei Lin is your Aunt. It just came out, and I hope I didn't create a problem."

"How did he react?"

"Startled as you would imagine but he seemed to be alright with it."

"How does he feel about me?"

"He wants to be your friend, and I asked him to ask you some personal questions to develop the friendship."

"That's great. Thank you. Have a good conversation at dinner but leave me out of it" and laughed.

59

Freedom Flight

When Joan arrived at school the next morning, she was surprised to see her new male classmate waiting for her. Apparently, he wasn't going to waste any time making his move.

"Hi Joan, I thought we could sit together in class."

"OK Fred, but don't think you can cheat by copying my notes.", and they both chuckled.

The instructor had much of the apparatus they would be using laid out on display. He proceeded to label each piece and describe its function. He passed out homework sheets and said: "Study these technical terms and be prepared to be tested on them tomorrow."

When exiting class, Fred suggested: "Let's have lunch and quiz each other on this homework."

"Fred, I would really like an honest answer. Do you want to study, or are you just hitting on me with male instinct?"

"Both! I do want to be 100 percent on that test tomorrow and rise to at least 75% in creating your interest in my male instincts."

"I don't yet know how smart you are; however, on the second part it is a long way from ten to seventy-five percent."

"Ten percent is much better than zero. It means I have a chance, even if slim. Hopefully, you will determine I am a "deeper" person than exclusively male instincts."

"I do like your self-confidence and green eyes. What motivated you to want to be a welder at this point in your life?"

"I sell new BMW's and have for ten years, and now would like to do something creative. I want to try welding sculptures."

Joan was mentally paralyzed for a few seconds.

"Fred, that is precisely my intention as well, although not to sell cars."

"You would probably be very good at selling cars. You exhibit loads of self-confidence and are obviously very smart, based on your ability to make interesting observations. It didn't take you very long to accurately assess my intentions and state your position. I find that very attractive and challenging. Most of the 'air-heads' I date are married and looking only for a sexual encounter, as their husbands are too busy making money to buy luxuries like a BMW. Emotionally the wives are hungry for male attention."

"Are you, or have you ever been, married?"

"No on both questions. My life has been consumed emotionally with a 'flavor of the month'."

"What flavor am I, not vanilla I hope?"

"Joan, you don't have a flavor, as you are too well developed to be given a label. I know you don't need my attention to add any fulfillment to your life: that is why I find you so attractive. Well, your beautiful face and perfect body also contributes to my attention."

"You are a smooth-talker. Probably make a lot of money selling lots of 'nice rides' and receiving a bonus from the buyers' wives when they take their ride."

"I do alright, but I don't feel fulfilled at age forty-two. Maybe, I have finally matured and seek satisfaction that money and sex don't provide."

"What kind of satisfaction would that be?"

"I think the answer is love. The only love I have ever felt is my mother's. I see her a couple times a week, and she always tells me to settle down and find love. She says: 'Before I die son, I want to see you in a loving relationship and a grandchild would be nice, also.' I am an only child and her only hope for that dream to come true. My father left us for another woman when I was six years old, and she raised me as a single mother. That is my story, tell me yours."

"I was a prostitute from age fourteen until nineteen. My mother was a prostitute. I have a six-year-old son and went to jail for two years. My son's father was one of my mother's 'Johns'. I have been out of jail for only a year and a half and am twenty-three years old. I am desperately trying to start over and be a good mother and provider. That should be enough information to erase your masculine instincts for me."

"Joan, I am not sure you are not making up a story just to eliminate my interest. However, it isn't working. If it is true, I admire your personal strength to be open and honest. I know I don't have

that much personal depth. I hope you will decide to give me an opportunity to tap into yours. Why did you go to jail and do you still
have contact with your son?"

"I am blessed to be able to have my son live with me now. Social
services had him while I was in jail. I stole money from my mother's
'Johns', at every opportunity. It was a plan she had concocted, and
it worked very well. While she engaged their total interest, I took
their car keys and robbed their money. Once I got greedy and took
a piece of jewelry as well. I pawned it without my mother's
knowledge, and the police found it when the 'John' turned in the
robbery. He didn't tell the police that he was screwing my mother
at the time."

"Joan, you may not believe this, but I am even more interested
in pursuing a relationship with you than I was before your story.
Your courage, given your early childhood environment, is a little
overwhelming. I would expect you to be a 'street woman', not a
welder."

"I am not a welder yet."

"No doubt you will be with your determination. Let's do some
studying. I want to weld with you. No pun intended: ha-ha."

"Fred, your 10% has already risen to 75%. Now let's pass the test
tomorrow."

60

The taxi pulled through the iron gates as an attendant stood by to provide access.

"Eleven ball in the corner", and then Robert Jr. was guided to the lobby and waited only a few moments for James's arrival. The other players were all arriving and went directly, as guided, to the recreation room. James greeted Robert, Jr. and asked: "Did Alice enjoy her sight-seeing?"

"Very much."

"She seems like a lovely and caring girl, and you are lucky you found her."

"I just found out today that I might not have found her if you had not made it possible. Do you know my mother?"

"Yes, I have met her. We need to go play pool; we can talk after the games."

The level of competition was very similar to two weeks earlier. James missed a makeable shot in the final game, as planned, and they got into a cab together without incident. Robert, Jr. wondered if the winners faced a robbery attempt. Maybe all of the players were "carrying".

James directed the cab to an upscale bar and said: "Let's drown our loss in a beer. It feels good to know that we could have won tonight. Robert, Jr., I knew your mother many years ago when I lived in Manhattan, and then lost touch when I moved to Chicago. I looked her up when I came back to Manhattan a couple of months ago. She told me about your life on the streets, and I asked her if I could try to connect with you. Meeting you was not an accident. Learning that you were an excellent pool player gave me the opportunity to befriend you. Something you should know: the money we win at pool is drug money. Nearly all those players are involved in large scale drug rings. They sit in their mansions and collect from the street dealers. They all have 'legit' businesses to cover how they really derive their income. When I recognized one of them making a phone call two weeks ago, I expected the robbery attempt. I continuously move our engagements to distant large cities to conceal our identities. When we win, we leave that city immediately after the game and make sure we are not followed. My law enforcement contacts alert me to where the games are being held. If you decide to continue as my partner, we will be flying all over the U.S. every few weeks."

"Can you tell me what your connection is with the law?"

"No, I cannot, and I must ask you not to tell anyone, not even Alice, about my connections."

Robert, Jr. paused for a moment in discomfort and then queried: "James, Alice has asked me not to keep secrets from her."

"I understand; however, my comfort with secrets is what you don't know, is not dangerous. I don't tell Evelyn about my activities, as it protects her from being a target. I don't put her in situations where the drug lords could connect her to me. I totally understand if you don't feel the same way. If you don't, I will find a new pool partner in some city."

Quickly, Robert, Jr. replied: "I want to be your partner. Alice likes you and she doesn't need to know everything, even though she thinks she does. James, can I ask you if you have ever been in love?"

"I have, only once."

"What did it feel like?"

"It felt like no other 'high' I have ever experienced. Playing pool, taking money from drug dealers, are nothing compared to being in love."

"What happened?"

"My way of life conflicted with the relationship and I had to flee, and that could happen again with Evelyn. I might be falling in love with her. Are you in love with Alice?"

"Based on your explanation, I am sure I am. I would rather be with Alice than even play pool. That is a totally new feeling for me."

"Don't fight it, Robert Jr. Just enjoy it as long as it lasts."

61

Connie was besieged with phone calls on Sunday evening. First Evelyn called, then James called, and even Robert, Jr. phoned. When Alice knocked on the door, Connie said: "Come in, I am talking to Robert, Jr."

"I wanted to tell you about the weekend. I guess you have heard most of it."

"No, I am sure there is news I haven't heard: sit down and I will get us some tea."

"The best news is that Robert is considering getting his high school diploma."

"Oh, Alice, that is wonderful news!"

"I told him I would help him study, so you will probably see him here often."

"The more the better. Thank you. James told me that Robert, Jr. knows I met him years ago."

"I didn't know that. I wonder how he feels about it. I will try to find out."

"You told him that Mei Lin is James's Aunt: how did he receive that news?"

"He was startled at first but seemed to be OK with it. He likes James and wants to be his friend."

"Connie, Robert, Jr. thinks he is in love with me and wants to marry me."

"How do you feel about him?"

"I think I am falling in love as well. No man has ever treated me with such respect and admiration. It feels really good: perhaps the best ever, to help him become the man I know he can be."

"James has certainly changed all of our lives after twenty-two years of disappointment. I guess I can finally forgive him. I want Robert, Jr. to know he is his father, but James will have to decide when the time is right. I hope he finds out before your wedding", and she smiled lovingly. "Don't be running off to Vegas: I want a church wedding so I can show everyone how proud I am of my son."

"I definitely want a church wedding, also. How was business at the shop while I was gone?"

"Quite good, Mei Lin helped me in your absence."

62

Robert, Jr. had a lot to think about. It still bothered him some that James and his mother had met many years earlier. He wondered if they had a romantic relationship. Mei Lin, being James's Aunt, and the new store opportunity: it was all too planned, but good. Why was James being so helpful? A relationship must have occurred, he thought. He was going to ask his mom about it.

After studying a history book with Alice one evening, he knocked on his mother's door.

"Hi, mom. I need to ask you something. Years ago, when you met James, were you involved?"

"He was close to your father and is being very kind to us."

Being purposefully misleading was not what she wanted to do, but it was James's request.

"He and Evelyn are getting quite close, also", he replied.

"Do you think they might get married? I know Evelyn would say yes, if he asked her, and she knows very little about his past or present. She has never even been to his residence, but she doesn't care. I would never do that, but she is happy, and I am happy for her. He treats her very well, and I hope that doesn't change. He could disappear just as quickly as he appeared. He seems to have too much money to just play pool. Evelyn says he invests in real estate in lots of different cities and that seems strange."

"Yes, he went early to both big money games. He said he had business to take care of."

"Robert, Jr., do you trust James?"

"I have no reason not to. He has been straight with me. I hope he marries Evelyn, and mom, I would like to marry Alice."

"Son, marriage is a very serious decision. I hope you do but please don't rush it. You need to know each other better. You have only known her for a few weeks."

"I feel like I know her very well already and you have known her for years."

"Yes, I have, and I know nothing at all negative about her. However, she probably doesn't know you well enough yet. What do you think you would like to do for work?"

"I've been thinking about that and nothing seems right."

"Well, it will come to you, just get that diploma. Then you can explore different things to see what you like."

"James suggested law enforcement but that doesn't feel right."

"Don't pressure yourself to do something that doesn't feel right: eventually something will."

"I hope so. Alice might not marry me until I have a job."

"Not to worry son, it will all work out."

63

Mei Lin opened the letter postmarked in China. It was from her brother, asking about the progress with Robert Jr.'s life. Having sold the car dealership, he now had time to pursue new endeavors. He was anxious to come back to the U.S. once Robert, Jr. knew he was his grandfather. He was his only grandchild, and he had never even met him.

Mei Lin wrote in return to Suh Yun about Robert, Jr.'s decisions and desire to get married. Perhaps you can attend a wedding when you visit the U.S. Suh Yun had returned to China, his birthplace, after Robert's mother passed away. She was an American Caucasian schoolteacher. They were married for eighteen years before she was diagnosed with cancer. They met in college and married immediately after graduation. Two years later, Robert was born. They named him Robert Young to preserve his American heritage. Both their names were pronounced similarly. Suh Yun worked for the FBI and was undercover in China identifying dirty money being laundered through the purchase of new cars. The vehicles were then shipped to the U.S. and sold, "cleaning" the drug money. The FBI could trace the money trail back to the U.S. while concealing Suh Yun's involvement.

64

Alice located a night school that would enable Robert to be a high school graduate. In as little as three months of study, he would qualify to take the examination. It was easier than he expected: of course, Alice was a big help. He had managed to control his lust and maintain a healthy balance while focusing on math and science. Both were subjects that posed little interest. The fact that caring touching always followed the study period was a motivating incentive. He had to purchase new boxer shorts more often now to replace the stained ones. With each purchase he was reminded that the reward far outweighed the cost. Despite his passion, he maintained his respect for Alice's wish to preserve her virginity. He was quite sure that might have been impossible for him, had she not permitted his sexual release. The frustration would have been intolerable. Cold showers and masturbation were less than fulfilling. That action was no longer necessary since falling in love with Alice.

Alice had reconsidered her decision after two months of dating Robert and feeling his pleasure. It wasn't fair, she thought, to make him feel such desire. She decided that her fingers massaging his penis were not violating her virginity: besides, she was curious and wanted to experience his masculinity with her touching. Now she felt even more pleasure in fulfilling his passion. She wanted him inside her; however, she didn't dare utter those words: that also would be unfair to him.

They discussed marriage plans often, and even solicited Connie's thought on the subject. All agreed that six months of dating, now every evening with the studying, should eliminate any surprises. A date was chosen in September before any chance of cold weather arriving.

Alice told Robert: "We will need to take classes at the Catholic Church before the priest will perform the ceremony. Will that bother you?"

"No, but I don't want him to think I am coming to his church every Sunday."

"Let him think what he wants, and you can do what you want. I know practicing religion is not on your priority list, and that is OK with me. However, if we have children and I hope we do, I want them to attend the church."

"Not a problem, religious training can't hurt them, and maybe it will keep them off the streets."

"Robert, our children will not be on the streets. They will have a loving and attentive father, unlike you did."

"Alice, I have been thinking that is a job I would like: taking kids off the streets. James did it for me, and without his attention, I would not have this great life. I want to do that for someone else."

"That is terrific, Robert! You need to study Sociology to get a good job doing that. After getting your diploma, you could attend the community college and major in that field. That knowledge will also make you a better father. Our children will benefit immensely since you didn't have a father to teach you. Oh, I am so happy, I could cry."

"Don't do that, I haven't done it yet, it is only an idea."

"Connie, Robert, Jr. wants to study sociology and take kids off the street."

Her early morning greeting was received with a question: "How did that happen?"

"It grew out of our conversation about raising our children."

"Wow! I am a grandmother already, and a few weeks ago I didn't feel like I was a mother. Please slow down and give me time to adjust. I am still looking for your wedding dress. By the way, one came in yesterday that you need to look at before we sell it. We also need to organize the guest list. A few are customers, who specifically asked to be invited. Have you written your parents to tell them?"

"Not yet, I won't until after the wedding. I am worried they might do something dumb."

66

Freedom Flight

"Can I call you Grandpa?"

"Sure Joseph, I would like to be your Grandpa. You would be my only grandson. I don't have any others. Would you like to watch a Disney movie on TV?"

"No, I would like to go fishing."

"I can't go today Joseph; I need to work on the book I am writing."

"Why are you writing a book?"

"To help people who have been treated unfairly. Do you like to help people?"

"No, I don't know how to help people."

"Well, it starts by being nice to them like Jenny and I did with your mom. She needed a friend and deserved one as her life had not been happy."

"I know she cried a lot, but she had lots of "uncles" that visited her. They were not her friends."

"They probably were not all nice people, and they only wanted to use your mother's kindness for their own pleasure. They were not trying to help her: real friends help. I can teach you how to help people, if you want me to."

"Sure, OK. I will watch a movie. Where is Jenny?"

"She went to the store to get groceries. I think she is going to buy that ice cream you like."

"Oh boy, I hope she gets home soon. When will mom get home from school? She told me we are going to the zoo tomorrow."

"I think she will be late today. She is studying with one of her classmates who has become a new friend."

"Does her new friend want to help her?"

"I hope so, or he wouldn't really be a friend, would he? We all need lots of friends to be a happy person. Are you making new friends at school?"

"Maybe, but I don't think they want to help me. Only Karen, she said she would help me talk to some other kids who don't talk to me."

"Why don't they want to talk to you? Are you nice to them, or do you treat them badly?"

"I don't know, they just walk right by me without looking at me."

"Maybe you need to start a conversation with them as they walk by, by smiling and asking them a question."

"They are not smiling at me."

"That is OK, someone has to smile first. Maybe they need a friend. Maybe they are afraid to smile because they think you won't smile back. It takes courage to be the first one to smile. Do you have courage?"

"What is courage, Grandpa?"

"It is being brave, Joseph."

"I am brave. I will fight with anyone, no matter how big they are."

"Joseph, courage is not about fighting, although fighting is sometimes impossible to avoid."

"What does that word mean?"

"What word?"

"That last one you said…. avoid?"

"Oh, a-v-o-i-d? Good question! That is a great way to learn, by asking questions. Well, let's see. Avoid means to not do it. If another boy is mean to you, and wants to fight, you can avoid him, or not fight him, by trying to be a friend to him. He probably needs a friend more than he needs a fight. Doing that is courage. Knowing you could fight him, but also knowing he needs a friend - making the right choice even though it is the harder thing to do. It would be easier to fight him than to be his friend. Deciding to be his friend takes even more courage than fighting him. However, if he hits you first, then you must hit him back. If he thinks you are afraid of him, he will probably never be nice to you or be your friend. Sometimes a fight can lead to a friendship if you think that is what he really needs. It is always worth trying."

"I want to watch the movie about Jack climbing the bean pole."

67

Freedom Flight

"Joseph is watching the bean stalk movie, Jenny. He is anxious to eat the ice cream. Were you able to find his favorite butter-scotch?"

"Yes, but I had to shop at two stores to find it."

"We had a long talk about friendship and courage. I don't know if he understood everything, I was trying to teach him. He asked me if he could call me Grandpa."

"Wow! That is great. I would like to be a Grandma, but I guess he has one of those. Even if he didn't understand all you told him, he probably got some of it. The next time he will get a little more. We think he is intelligent, and eventually his 'Grandpa's' words will be important to him. Every boy needs a Grandpa, and you are doing a wonderful thing by taking the time to explain things to him. He has never known that before. My psychology classes taught me that explaining things in conversation, especially feelings, is the most important element in a rewarding relationship."

"Have you met Jenny's new male friend from school?"

"Not yet but she asked me if she could bring him here some day after school. Of course, I said yes. I want to assess his intentions. Is he really interested in her as a person, or only her very attractive body? I hope he isn't lying to her about being single. She doesn't need another deception at this point in her resurrected life. She has a strong fortitude fortunately but could lose her faith in humanity with another let-down. If she didn't have Joseph, I suspect she would still be living as a prostitute. It would be a lot easier to survive not trusting anyone. I also suspect that is the reason why most women remain in the world's "oldest profession'. Their earlier environment taught them to 'take rather than give'." We both should feel very worthwhile that she recognized something in us that generated her trust. I do think initially she only planned to 'take' from our good nature. She thought she was 'playing' us by behaving as a caring mother. When she became convinced that we truly wanted to provide caring affection for Joseph, she developed trust in us. I believe her trust in us is still fragile, and we must be careful not to do or say anything to fracture her confidence in us. It would be devastating to Joseph to lose his Grandpa."

"Jenny, where did you develop that wealth of insight?"

"My own deficient early environment left me with a lot of 'scars'. I didn't trust people who might have become friends. When I moved to Chicago, I realized that my insecurities needed to be addressed. I went to night school one night a week for ten years, studying psychology. I never intended to practice it, only to personally benefit from what I learned. Now maybe I can practice it with Joan and Joseph. The knowledge of understanding individuals' personal psychological needs and then addressing those needs is very fulfilling.

"Jenny, you have provided that positive influence on me, as well. My bitterness when I left prison was 'all consuming'. I might never have changed that orientation without your devoted understanding. Most likely, I would have never found happiness. Why didn't you want to practice professionally the great skill you have to offer?"

"Jeffrey, I remain a victim of my childhood. I am fearful of rejection when I am put in a position of engaging in meaningful conversation with a stranger. Honestly, when I met you for the first time at the jail, I had confidence only because I knew you probably wouldn't reject me. You would want to take advantage of my apparent vulnerability. It gave me an opportunity to gain your trust and acceptance of me while you were only 'using' me for your own satisfaction. I could use my psychology knowledge without fear of your rejection."

"It worked perfectly, and it turns me on. Let's get in the shower. I want to enjoy your wet body, every inch of it. Conversation is great foreplay: I am already wet."

68

"James, I know you have a secret life, and that is OK with me, but do you think we could ever live together with your secrets?

She had been thinking about asking him this question since they returned from the Philadelphia weekend two weeks earlier. She knew asking was risky but couldn't help herself. James didn't appear surprised by the question, she thought.

"Evelyn, are you in love with me, or just prefer my being with you? There is a big difference."

"Yes, James. I fell in love, but not out of lust, while we were in Philadelphia,"

"Why haven't you told me?"

"If you don't feel the same way, it would scare you off," she replied.

"I do feel the same way and want to live with you after we are married."

Evelyn couldn't believe what she was hearing: he was proposing marriage! She was truly speechless and couldn't speak a word.

Finally, he asked: "What does your silence mean?"

"It means I had never even thought about you asking me to marry you. Of course, I will."

He questioned her further: "You do realize that I will be gone, sometimes for a week, and can't always tell you where I am."

"I do."

"Are you practicing your wedding vows?"

They both laughed and she went to his arms and they kissed with love. They were sitting at a bar when this life changing conversation took place. Evelyn wished they were at home. She wanted to make love to him.

She asked: "How should we celebrate this decision?"

"In your bed", he replied.

The bird flew higher than ever as if it would never touch land again. Then it flew again and again before she offered: "how do you want your eggs this morning?"

"Scrambled, like my mind", he replied.

This proposal had not been planned just yet, but he was glad it happened. He had never been married and never expected to be. The realization of marriage was still developing as he sipped the morning coffee.

"Evelyn, we have a lot to discuss before we make plans for our wedding."

"Are you having second thoughts?" she responded.

"No, I want to marry you, but my life is complicated and everything I have told you is not accurate."

"By accurate, you mean you have told me lies?"

"I don't like that word although I am feeling some discomfort."

"James, I do love you and I can live with you misleading me. I don't need to know the truth about your life. I only need your love: please forget your discomfort. I want you to always feel only comfort with our relationship. My life has been loveless for a long time and finding you has been the best thing that ever happened to me. I need to share some discomfort, also."

"What is that?"

"My two children."

"I don't understand", he replied.

"My son and daughter both use drugs, and their lives are a mess. I don't want that to become your problem or affect our relationship."

"Have you told them that you are involved with me?"

"No, I don't discuss my life with them. Honestly, I only talk to them when they contact me for money."

"Evelyn, I have been around a lot of drug use and that life is not foreign to me. Don't tell them about us and give me their names and addresses if you are OK with that."

69

James called Robert, Jr. and told him the next pool engagement would be on Saturday, in ten days: Evelyn and Alice would not be able to accompany them to Miami. The agenda was the same, they would meet at the hotel; however, he was to meet James the previous Wednesday. They drove to a private gun range and James handed him a Glock revolver.

"You need to be familiar with this, in the event you ever need to use it."

In the Miami hotel room, James once again handed him the Glock and a holster to wrap around his right leg: just above the ankle.

"Robert, Jr., put one of these gloves in each of your jacket pockets."

With packed bag, he climbed in the Corvette Z as they departed the hotel. Robert, Jr. looked at the speedometer.

"Do you expect to peg this thing?"

"No, but it would outrun most 'bad guys' cars."

The host home had large columns about two hundred yards inside the Iron Gate. It was built to resemble a southern plantation. After announcing "Three Ball in the Middle", they parked adjacent to the columns and were directed to an elevator. Surprisingly, they exited the fourth floor in the middle of a pool room. Ten tables surrounded the elevator and the players were hanging their sports jackets on the close rack. Twenty teams meant twice the competition and a $100,000 purse. Robert, Jr. was surprised that the competition was not as talented as he had seen in Pittsburgh and Philadelphia: mostly he observed huge egos who acted like they were much better than their skills demonstrated. Only the final few challengers presented any real threat of losing. It was James this time who made the inconceivable 'jump-shot' paving the way to victory. James took his time stashing the cash inside his sport coat while the final competitors were exiting in the elevator. When they were the only ones remaining, he told James to put on the gloves and take out the revolver.

"It is possible we may have to shoot our way out of here. If my plan works, that won't be necessary. Just follow my lead and stay close, always to my right."

James pushed the elevator button and then went around the elevator shaft to a closet door on the back side and went inside. They stepped onto a "dumb-waiter" platform, and then grabbed the steel cable and James took out his phone.

"Go", he directed. Then a second call: "Coming down."

They exited underground in a wine cellar and were met by another gun toting middle aged man. All three ran through the cellar to steps leading to a back street. They jumped in an older Impala and followed a small truck being led by an older Buick. Once on the way, Robert, Jr. asked: "What about the Vette?"

"It is no doubt being followed as we speak", was the reply.

The three-vehicle convoy remained on city streets and proceeded to Fort Lauderdale. The cars parked by the dock and the truck drove onto the gangplank and stopped aboard a small cargo boat. The truck driver ran to one of the waiting cars while Robert, Jr. and James and the truck motored out of the harbor. The boat captain remarked: "Is the cargo all aboard?"

James responded: "Let's look."

They opened the truck back door and James offered: "There are six paintings worth six million dollars that were loaded from the house while we were playing pool for $95,000, a profitable night I would say, and we didn't need the revolvers. That drug dealer won't be wearing a smiley face tomorrow."

Robert, Jr. wasn't sure if he was an accomplice wanted by the law or a Robin Hood in service to the good of mankind. He did know it was an experience he would not share with Alice.

70

Freedom Flight

"Joan, other than Jeffrey, you are my only friend. I have never made friends as you know from our many in-depth conversations. I really value your friendship, and I would like to share a secret burden that I am carrying heavily. I need to tell somebody. Every day it bothers me more, and I really need to let it out."

"Absolutely, Jenny. You can tell me anything. Even if you murdered someone, I would still be your confidante and friend just as you have been for me."

"I am the person who put Jeffrey in jail."

Joan's eyes immediately became glazed.

"What do you mean? Why? How?"

"It was pure selfishness. I wanted to be the woman in his life, and he didn't know I existed. I even stalked him and watched his every pattern of behavior. He didn't have a serious female relationship. In the ten years I watched, only infrequent chance encounters. Other than work, he didn't have male friends to pal around with. I thought we were perfect for each other, and I fell in love with him without ever talking to him. I know that is extremely abnormal and knew it at the time, but I needed the relationship even if only in my mind. I couldn't approach him because I knew he would reject me. I am not a beautiful woman and have always known that, since as a little girl, my father always told me. One day it occurred to me that 'trapping' him would be my only chance of capturing him. Some women 'capture' by getting pregnant. Finally, after ten years of yearning for his attention, it came to me. Bank embezzlement would put him in jail, and then I could rescue him. It was easy to put my plan into action. Working at the same bank, I had access to his account. I wrote a check for $5,000 every month to a fictitious charity that I set-up. The check, of course, was allegedly signed by him from the bank's own account. It was easy to study his signature and create the forgery. I deposited the checks in an offshore personal account which still exists. When caught, I expected him to serve only two to three years in an 'executive' confinement. The hard-core judge sentenced him to six years locked up with murderers and rapists and who knows what else. I was sickened when I read the sentence. I took a six-month leave of absence and drowned in my sorrow. After recovering somewhat, I decided to continue with my plan by writing him letters. I even sent him a picture of a beautiful woman to capture his interest. The plan worked, and he answered every letter. I knew he thought I was a vulnerable 'air-head' and that was alright because he was now in my life."

"How did he get caught?"

"After six years, a bank auditor finally checked the charity and couldn't determine its validity. I thought they would find it the first year. I didn't expect to wait for six years before he was caught. Foreign transactions are more time consuming to audit, and they just didn't take the time necessary to do a thorough audit. I have $360,000 to withdraw. However, I can't put it in my bank, and I don't want it under my pillow. It is a dilemma. The pain that I have caused Jeffrey is what really elevates my blood pressure. I no longer have a psychologically distorted attraction for him. Now I have real true love for him. He has the character and kindness I always suspected. Watching him with Joseph only increases my awareness of his goodness. He gives of himself so freely, despite having endured prison life that he didn't deserve."

"Jenny, I am truly in shock. If I wasn't aware of your character, I wouldn't believe your story. It is almost too bizarre to be true. Your childhood generated even more damage than mine. I preyed on men's desire for pleasure and took their money but I can't begin to imagine how much you are hurting for your need to find companionship with a man, and then to fall in love with him must be like living with a knife in your heart. You know I will keep your secret, but you took a big risk by telling me. You know, there is money available for identifying criminals and the court would require the bank, due to their neglect, to pay Jeffrey for those six years of incarceration, and it would be a lot more than $360,000."

"I know, and I am going to tell Jeffrey what I've done. It is the only way to take the knife out of my heart. That is why I am telling you first. You can turn me in and collect the reward. Jeffrey will live as a wealthy man for the rest of his life, and I will get relief from my painful guilt."

"Jenny, that is total nonsense! Jeffrey's pain is over. He suffered and endured. He is a happier man now than he was before prison. If he found out what you did, his happiness would probably turn to anger again. No doubt he would feel betrayed. I can see he loves you and his loss would only cause him agonizing misery. Think about what it would do to Joseph's life if his 'grandpa' became an angry man. He would lose his chance to be psychologically normal. Jeffrey and you have given him a chance to develop into a healthy adult. You are erasing his scar tissue, which I generated. A confession to Jeffrey would destroy any chance I have of being a good mother. If Joseph goes back into his shell, I will be helpless to find him again. Your confession would negatively affect three lives, and one of those lives is only six years old. I know you are hurting badly. However, it is better that you hurt the rest of your life than hurting three others for the rest of their lives. Just suck-up your pain and keep providing happiness to our lives. That is how you can pay your debt."

71

Connie, Evelyn and Alice spent that Saturday night at Connie's apartment, and Alice appreciated the hair styling. When their discussion revealed the advent of two weddings:

Connie offered: "Why not a party for four? You could both be married in one ceremony. For sure, James would want to attend Robert, Jr.'s wedding. I do hope James tells him before September."

Evelyn quickly responded: "Sounds good to me", and Alice contributed her own positive sentiment.

"How will we tell the boys about this idea?" Alice questioned.

"I think it is time we all had dinner together and we will include Mei Lin", was Connie's response.

Alice then questioned: "Evelyn, do you know anything about James's life other than he plays pool very well?"

"Only that he told me he has other sources of income and that he expects me to live without asking about his secrets."

"Are you comfortable with that?" Alice responded.

"Absolutely, I only care about him being in my life. I don't care what else he does."

"I couldn't live that way, and have told Robert, Jr. how I feel."

Connie interceded: "Let's hope James is an undercover FBI agent, just as he was when he was known as Robert Young. Although from what you have told me, Evelyn, he seems to have too much money for that livelihood."

"Remember he said he sold his father's car dealership in China. I don't know about China but in the U.S., that could be millions of dollars", Alice countered.

"All we can do is cross our fingers. I don't want my son involved with anything illegal, and he most likely was before James suddenly became part of our lives."

"Let's plan our big event," Evelyn suggested.

"<u>Where</u> is the first thing to determine, I would think." replied Connie.

"I am going to get married in a Catholic church, and Robert, Jr. is OK with that. Is James Catholic?"

"I have no idea; we have never discussed religion. Being in a bedroom most of the time hasn't aroused <u>that</u> point", and then she laughed out loud. "I don't care myself, but I will ask him."

"My priest will probably not marry you unless one of you is Catholic. However, we could still have our reception dinner together. Robert, Jr. and I don't have many guests."

"I don't have many, either, but I did tell James about Jeff and Amanda when he proposed. Hearing about their drug habits, he asked me for their addresses. I don't know why, and I didn't ask. If he plans to try to help them like he did Robert, Jr., that's great. If he plans to arrest them, perhaps that is the best for them."

Connie responded immediately: "I doubt he would have them arrested but let's talk about where we should have the dinner. It is not too early to make reservations."

"I don't want Chinese," Alice responded and all three laughed.

72

Mei Lin locked the dry-cleaning store and took the subway downtown. When she approached the restaurant, James beckoned her to follow him. Without a greeting, she followed inconspicuously at a half block's length. James hailed a cab which drove around the block and then stopped to permit Mei Lin to join him. Not a word was spoken until they exited the cab and entered a very small café. Sitting in a back booth, with James facing the door, he spoke:

"Sorry to ask you to meet me but I have news to tell you."

"No trouble?" she responded.

"Can't talk at your place…too close to Connie and Alice. Robert, Jr. accompanied me during the painting robbery in Miami. As we expected, he handled the situation without exhibiting any anxiety. Tell dad he passed with flying colors. Also, I asked Evelyn to marry me. It is a risk, but I think she can handle not knowing about my life."

"James, your father will be disappointed. Too dangerous. Memory of first wife's death very strong."

"I know. Tell him he will need to trust my judgment. I believe Evelyn would accept the risk if she knew, rather than lose our love. Even one more day together would be her choice, and mine also."

"When is wedding?"

"We haven't decided yet. I would like dad to be here. Ask him if he can come."

Immediately when getting home, Mei Lin wrote to Suh Yun as James asked. She was not looking forward to his reply.

73

Freedom Flight

"Fred, I would like you to meet the people who gave me new life. Jenny and Jeffrey, I would like you to meet Fred. He is a man who is either disturbed to want my companionship or brilliant to recognize what I have to contribute to his life."

"Wow Joan, it is terrific to hear you describe me in such endearing terms. What about the absolute enrichment I can bring to your life? You didn't know anything about BMW's before you met me."

All four got a good chuckle and Jenny responded: "I think brilliant is the more accurate option. Pleased to meet you Fred and Joan you do have a lot to contribute. She has been as valuable to our lives as she gives us credit for helping her. She recognizes future results that are blind to us normal beings", and Joan gave Jenny a warm smile. She knew what Jenny was referring to.

"Fred, welcome to our somewhat unusual group, and none of us know anything about BMW's. You still need to meet the light of our group. He is in the back-yard practicing casting for fly fishing. We are going tomorrow. Do you fish?"

"Never have but I would like to learn."

"I am certain Joseph would enjoy teaching you. I will get him. Joseph, this man's name is Fred. He is a new friend of your mother's. He wants to learn how to fish, and I thought you might want to teach him when I am busy working on my book."

"Sure, I can do that. I am getting good at casting. It just takes a little practice. Come out in the yard and I will show you."

Fred promptly followed Joseph out the door.

"Well Joan, he certainly makes a good first impression. He knows how to tune-into individuals' interests. I guess that is why he is a good BMW salesman."

"Yes, Jenny and he tuned-into me immediately. When I told him about my history, he never blinked. I expected him to avoid me forever. He has had lots of female conquests, and I certainly was not a sexual opportunity for him. Dating an ex-prostitute does pose a risk, and even realizing that risk, he continued to pursue me. I knew then his character values interested me. We have studied together six times and he hasn't made any advance sexually. We haven't even kissed."

"Do you plan to kiss him ever?"

"I wanted him to meet Joseph before we begin any romantic involvement. If he bonds with Joseph, rather than just accept him as part of my life, I do want to give him pleasure. I thought the wait might deter his interest. His patience has made him even more attractive. I am hoping Joseph likes him, because I do."

"How is he doing in welding school?"

"We haven't actually started welding yet. That commences next week. He has passed all of his written tests. He is smart enough. Neither one of us know how we will do when we light the torch, no pun intended."

Jeffrey had been listening as the two women conversed and decided to enter the fray.

"Well, in my opinion, you have kept him waiting too long already. He may have concluded that you have no interest in sexual relations, given your history. He needs to find his satisfaction some place. Do you care if he is dating other women while pursuing you? That is a formula for losing him. Anyway, that is my male perspective."

"Yes Jeffrey, I do care, and I thought my goal was worth the risk. He may be dating, I don't know. His interest is strong enough, far beyond flirting, that I decided on a plan that puts Joseph as number one priority."

"Well, they seem to be off to a good beginning."

"Yes, I am pleased. I will measure Fred's sincere interest in Jeffrey when we talk tonight. If I am convinced, he is going to be a caring mentor, I think our first kiss may be in order."

74

James sat in an old Dodge and watched Jeff leave the low-income housing project. It was about 2 P.M. on a Wednesday, and he had been eye-balling the place since 7 A.M. Being restless after seven hours in that cramped space, he was glad to see Jeff emerge. He followed him on foot for six blocks and stopped short when he entered a bar on Twenty Second Street: waited five minutes, and then entered. Jeff was sitting on a stool with a beer in hand. James sat on the adjacent bar stool and immediately introduced himself.

"Hello Jeff, I am James."

Startled, he replied: "How do you know me?"

"I don't really. I only know your name, and I am going to marry your mother. Thought we should get to know each other."

"Don't expect me to like you just because you are going to be my step-father."

"I don't care if you like me or not, but you are going to respect me and your mother and attend our wedding without being under the influence."

"And if I don't?"

"I will have your dealer on First Street arrested. I believe he goes by the name of Mike and plays pool at Angelo's on Fourth Street. Further, I will tell him you gave me his name."

"Are you a cop?"

"Doesn't make any difference…I can arrange the arrest and make your worthless life miserable. You have a choice: you can clean-up your act with my help or elevate your misery. Bartender, give this man another beer and I will have the same. How would you like to make $5,000 in the next two weeks?"

"Robbing who?"

"Robbing yourself of the addiction. I will take you right now to a place to rehab, not tomorrow, and you stay two weeks and I will give you $5,000 when you get out."

"I am supposed to trust a stranger for $5,000?"

"No, you call your mother at the hair salon and tell her we are coming over. Tell her you need to confirm my identity through the window. Ask her if I am good for the money: certainly, you can trust your mother. An easy choice. The drug gang ends your life, or you get $5,000. Either way, your mother comes out ahead and that is my only interest. When you exit rehab, I will have a job for you. If you don't stay clean until after the September wedding, the dealer arrest stands. After the wedding, you are on your own. You can be a worthwhile son or continue being a disappointment to your mother. By the way, if you stay clean, and I will know, there is an additional $10,000 coming."

After registering Jeff in the rehab, James went directly to Evelyn's apartment.

"How did you convince him to rehab?"

"Just a little persuasive threatening. Don't get your hopes up: he may not make it. You can 'lead a horse to water but you can't make him drink'."

"Thanks, James, for trying."

"Tomorrow I intend to have a conversation with Amanda so tell me about her."

"She is twenty-two years old, single, no children and lives with a boyfriend."

"Is he also a druggie?"

"Yes, and I think he is a gang member."

"What gang?"

"I don't know."

It wasn't long before they were peeling each other's clothes off and enjoying their loving lust. She could never get enough of tasting him, and he could never get enough of her tongue devouring him.

Amanda's boyfriend was pure scum, as James determined by observing his behavior for two days. The boyfriend would need to be taken out of the picture before he approached Amanda. On the third day, he was picked up by Drug Enforcement while 'buying'. The seller was also removed from the street. The dealer was identified and charged. His attorney arranged bail, and he continued to live in his mansion with possessions purchased with laundered drug money. A house ripe for a robbery: all it needed was a "For-Sale" sign.

James watched Amanda's comings and goings for ten days before he thought he knew her vulnerabilities. She hung-out with the other girls who worked at the donut factory. They made donuts: didn't sell them. She was becoming more anxious each day as her boyfriend had purchased the drugs, and she didn't know the source. Being "strung out" wasn't becoming, and her friends commented to her about her looks and demeanor.

"Evelyn, can you phone Amanda and ask her to come over for dinner tonight? Tell her you want her to meet me. Be prepared, she will be nervous as she hasn't had a 'fix' in ten days."

"Amanda, this is James, my intended in September: thought you should meet the man who is going to be your step-father."

"Hello, James."

"Nice to meet you, Amanda. Obviously, you inherited your mother's good looks."

Amanda did not respond. They sat down to a plate of spaghetti: Evelyn never claimed to be good in the kitchen. The store-bought sauce was not appetizing as James determined with the first fork full. Looks like I will be doing the cooking, he surmised.

"Amanda, Evelyn tells me you work at a donut factory. How do you like your job?"

"It is sweet", she responded without thought, as apparently, she had answered that question before.

"What are your favorite things to do when you are not working?"

Amanda's body language exhibited her discomfort with the questions.

"I am tired when I get home from work and don't do anything."

It was obvious to James that she wasn't enjoying life, and no doubt, that contributed to her use of drugs.

"Your mother says you have a boyfriend. Is it serious?"

"We are not together anymore. Can we talk about something else, instead of me?"

"Sure, I just wanted to get to know you as a person rather than only a name in my family. I know a young man who would like to meet a 'sweet' woman. He is a cop and doesn't see much sweetness all day. Maybe you two would enjoy each other's company. I've been told he is a good dancer: could I introduce you?"

Amanda relaxed her stiff body a little and said: "He probably wouldn't like me. I haven't danced since high school."

"I will take that as a qualified yes: worst case, you don't like each other and you have only lost two hours in which you weren't doing anything, anyway. I will set it up."

Amanda left early after leaving most of her spaghetti on the plate, and seemingly disturbed.

"Evelyn, I apologize for upsetting her, although, in her condition that may have been inevitable."

"Never you mind. Are you really going to set up a blind date?"

"Yes, she must break free from her current environment to have a chance of breaking the addiction. A new boyfriend could possibly give her a 'natural high' to replace her artificial one."

Evelyn replied: "Do you think she will come to the date?"

"It is probably 50-50 at best, but if she doesn't, we will need to take more direct action; that is, if you want to."

"James, I trust your judgment and we have nothing to lose. By the way, are you Catholic?"

"I was raised Buddhist but haven't practiced religion in a long time. Why do you ask?"

Connie and Alice would like a Catholic double wedding, and one of us needs to be Catholic."

"I like the double wedding idea and, sure, I will be Catholic for a day. We will need to attend a Catholic service and practice."

75

Freedom Flight

"Joan, your son certainly has an engaging personality. He just bubbles over with enthusiasm for life. He talks non-stop about his grandpa."

"Yes, I am amazed. If you had met him three months ago, he wouldn't have spoken to you. He didn't speak to anyone. I thought I had created a child who would be psychologically handicapped for life. Living on the streets didn't give me the opportunity to spend much time with him. Social services only granted one-hour visits twice a week. They were supervised, and I couldn't be alone with him. It was a very 'stiff' and artificial setting for a mother and son: not that I didn't deserve it. When Jeffrey first mentioned fishing, it rivaled a miracle. It was like a baby bird breaking its shell and seeing the world for the first time. He put his absolute trust in Jeffrey, from the moment he met him. None of the men he had ever met before were even conscious or cared that he existed. Maybe Jeffrey's attention and expressed interest broke his shell. Fred, I can't allow a man's betrayal of interest to disturb Joseph's portrait of men now. Can you understand that?"

"Joan, I am not a betrayal natured person. Yes, I have not lived a productive life but rather a selfish one. However, I have always been honest about who I was. If you can believe it, I have never told a woman in my life that I loved her. I didn't, and I wouldn't, misrepresent myself just to get her in bed. I realized I had to look in the mirror and not be ashamed of what I saw. A betrayal would make me feel ashamed. More than one married woman has confused 'smitten lust' for love. When I recognized that, I ended the affair abruptly. I told them I wasn't in love, and to continue the affair would only hurt them. They were already hurt, but not intentionally by me. They had expressed the initial interest, not the other way around. Most of them only wanted sex with a younger man who they found attractive. I was more than willing to get my pleasure while satisfying their interests. I never betrayed one of them. Being honest about my feelings gives me a clear conscience. However, in essence, I was just as much a prostitute as you. I can commit to you that I would never betray Joseph or you, regardless of how our relationship evolves. I would only develop my bonding with Joseph as his friend: nothing more unless my relationship with you develops with mutual love, and you want Joseph to have a 'Grandpa' and a father."

"Do you really want to be a father?"

"I have always wanted to have my own children someday. I have never thought about being a stepfather. For now, I would just like to be Joseph's friend and your exclusive boyfriend."

"Does that mean you are willing to give up the BMW wives for me?"

"Joan, they don't mean anymore to me than sex. Of course, I would forego that pleasure. I wouldn't want or need it if I were having great sex with you while pursuing love. Lots of men need multiple sex partners to fill their conquest needs. I have never sought conquests, only pleasure."

"Fred, I am not sure how 'great' the sex will be with me. My experience in bed has only been a monetary desire. I have never expected pleasure and have never experienced it. In that respect, I am a virgin. I don't know if I can derive pleasure from sex, and it concerns me a great deal when contemplating a relationship with you."

"Joan, honestly, that makes me want you even more. I am 'hard' right now and would like to take you to bed. However, I don't want our first time to be a result of my lust. You might not feel my deeper feelings for you. I want you to feel my interest in you as a person before you feel my physical desire. When we 'do it', I want my interest in you to be an all-consuming desire that you have never felt previously. If and when you get that feeling, you tell me and then we will find out if you derive pleasure. In the meantime, but not forever, I will give myself a 'hand job' after our time together generates my desire. No more BMW encounters."

Robert wasn't apprehensive about the test as Alice had thoroughly prepared him. He felt she was really smart and knew what would be on the test. He learned more from her than the night school courses.

"Robert, you need a good night's sleep tonight to be rested for the test in the morning."

"Alice, I always feel rested in the morning after spending the evening with you. You relieve my tension from studying and memorizing."

With those words, he placed his lips ever so lightly on hers and inserted his tongue. She had taught him how to kiss with passion. Feeling his tongue, she put her hand in his boxer shorts and pulled his foreskin back and forth very slowly. She made him wait before increasing her hand speed to create the explosion.

"Now, go home and go to bed. Good luck in the morning."

Nothing on the test was surprising although he knew he had forgotten the meaning of some words. The math questions he found easy, nothing to memorize. Within two hours, the computer cranked out the testing facility's results, as he waited.

"Robert, Jr., you made 85%, congratulations!"

"Thank you", he responded as he firmly held his written accomplishment.

It felt even better than he had expected, perhaps as good as winning at pool. He went immediately to the dress shop but not before stopping at the florist. He bought two bouquets.

"The flowers must mean good news", Alice responded.

"Eighty five percent!" Robert, Jr. replied.

"I am so proud of you son, how thoughtful to get the flowers."

"I could not have done it without you two."

"You did a better job than you thought, Connie. He has love and appreciation in his heart."

"I had no idea it would feel this good to hold this piece of paper. Now I do want that sociology you talked about, Alice."

"You know, Robert, Jr., that education sounds good to me, also: maybe I will go with you." Connie relayed. "I would like to understand the political system."

"I want to study sociology with Robert, Jr.", countered Alice. "Seems like this group will be busy studying after the weddings in September."

77

"Eddie, can you have coffee with me in the morning when your shift ends?"

"I can do that, James. What's up? You need dirt on a bad guy?"

"Not this time, it is better than that."

Eddie had been a "beat" cop in Manhattan for eight years and was respected by his fellow officers, and they would like for him to have their backs. He had served for six years on the battlefield with the U.S. Marine Corps and had received the Medal of Honor for bravery. James was confident that Eddie would not be intimidated by a young woman who used drugs. He was divorced two years ago after a marriage of only one year. He was an open book to his peers, and they all knew about the details of his life.

"Amanda, this is Eddie-the man I told you about. Eddie, this is Amanda-my intended's beautiful daughter. She gets her looks from her mother. I can't add anything to your conversation, so I am leaving."

James had arranged the introduction at 10 A.M. on a Sunday morning at a coffee shop.

"You are beautiful, Amanda, just like James promised. It is my pleasure to meet you."

Amanda only weakly smiled, preserving her resistant manner.

"How should we start, you choose", he offered.

"Why did you agree to meet me: just because James told you I was beautiful?"

"You're right. If he had told me you were ugly, I wouldn't be here."

"At least you are honest, and I expect you're planning on sex."

"I certainly would not say no but I would like to know about your life before we go there."

"My life is prioritized by getting high. You are a cop, and you know where to get it, and that is why I am here."

"Can't get any more honest and direct than that: drugs followed by sex. Sounds good to me. I will meet you at 6:00 P.M. at your place.

Eddie had not known what to expect but it was certainly not this. He was sure it wasn't what James had in mind, either. When he was off duty, he occasionally used recreational marijuana and indulging with Amanda was an easy choice given the anticipated pay-off. He was on a three day off-duty schedule and could get it out of his system by Wednesday.

Sunday evening and night and Monday were not a disappointment for either Eddie or Amanda. They remained high and nude for the duration. Amanda climaxed with each ejaculation which occurred more frequently than Eddie had ever previously experienced. He stopped counting when he ran out of fingers.

78

Freedom Flight

"Grandpa, why don't we eat the fish that we catch?"

"Well, Joseph, it just takes a long time to clean them. You have to take all that outside skin off."

"I have lots of time. Show me how to do it."

"Come over here to the sink, and we will clean one," Jenny offered.

"Are you sure you know how to do it?"

"Oh, yes. When I was a little girl, I cleaned all the fish my father brought home."

We didn't have much money, and we ate everything he caught or shot."

"Why didn't you have much money?'

"Well, my father wasted the money he had by drinking alcohol. His drinking was like a sickness. That is why you should never even taste one drink of alcohol. It could give you the sickness."

"I don't think I will taste it. I don't like to be sick. I can't go fishing."

"Jenny, I would like you to read what I wrote this morning. I like it but I need your honest opinion to tell me what you think."

"Sure, Jeffrey and I think you should get Joan's opinion, also."

"What I wrote was about Joan and Joseph. It might be too personal for her."

"Let me read it and decide if I think Joan can handle it. She is a very strong young woman. She is good at separating emotion from decision-making. The way she has managed her relationship with Fred has amazed me, and she has even given me some helpful advice about our relationship."

"What advice was that?"

"Oh, just women stuff. Nothing that a man wants to hear or should hear. I am sure men talk about their wives and girlfriends to other men and say things that a woman should never hear. Now the fish is ready to cook, Joseph, and I am going to sit down and read what Jeffrey wrote."

"When I first met Joan, she was obviously a hurting person. She had been in prison for two years and living on the street for six months. She was very distraught when I first met her, and I could see remnants of tears on her cheeks. Despite her unkempt appearance, I could sense a kind and helpful spirit. It seemed her spirit remained imprisoned and was searching for a 'freedom flight'. I, myself, could easily find empathy as I also felt like my spirit was in need of flight when I emerged from my incarceration. She, surprisingly, was open to talking with me about her situation. My significant other wanted to meet her, and seemingly impulsively invited her into her home. She was taking a large risk, not knowing anything about Joan's character. Joan told us she had a six-year old son who was a ward of Social Services. That young man, Joseph, has become the 'highlight' of my life. I would have never met Joseph if I had not been wrongfully convicted of embezzlement. The universe works in mysterious ways."

As she read, Jenny had a difficult time hiding her erupting emotions. Her guilt was ebbing and submerging like a floating piece of wood in the rapids.

<h1 style="text-align:center">79</h1>

The marriage reservations were finalized, and September 25th was selected as the foursome "tee-off" to a new life.

Mei Lin received an answer from Suh Yun: he would arrive on the day prior to the weddings and leave on September 26th. Surprisingly, he did not mention any concerns about James getting married. He did request that his grandson be apprised of their relationship prior to his arrival. He also inquired concerning an appropriate wedding gift.

Mei Lin contacted James and communicated Suh Yun's wishes.

"That puts some pressure on me to tell Robert, Jr. I hope he is ready for the surprise.

"He is ready", Mei Lin responded. "No worry."

James wasn't nearly as confident as his aunt. He needed to discuss his intentions with Connie. She might have some strong feelings about the presentation.

"Connie, I need to talk to you about my father. I can't come over; Robert Jr. might see me. Can you come to Evelyn's place tonight?"

"Certainly, what time?"

James arrived early at Evelyn's, and they had dessert before dinner. James then prepared salmon which he had picked up at his favorite fresh fish market. When Connie arrived, she seemed a bit frazzled.

"Connie is something wrong?" queried Evelyn.

"Oh, I just witnessed a shooting on the way over. It was upsetting, to say the least".

"Was anyone killed?" James inquired.

"It looked like there was. A young person wearing a hood walked up to an older man and shot him in the face."

"Were you close enough to see his face?"

"Yes, he passed by me before he shot."

"Have you talked to the Police?"

"No, I came directly here."

"Did he see your face?"

"I don't think so. He was looking down."

"Did you look to make sure you were not followed?"

"No, but I am sure I wasn't. He ran off after shooting."

"Connie, his accomplice could have seen you and followed you here. They usually work in pairs", and James went to the window to observe the street.

"Evelyn, have you ever seen that black Ford parked there before?"

"No, I have never noticed it."

James pulled out his cell phone: "This is James Whitmore, is Eddie Mitchell on duty?"

He waited and then said: "Good, have him call me immediately." When his phone rang, he answered: "Hello, Eddie. Come to the corner of Madison and Second Street. I will meet you there."

When James and Eddie and another cop approached the suspicious vehicle, they saw two men in the front seat. Coming from behind the car, they were not noticed. Eddie, in uniform, announced: "Get out of the car, hands on your head." The man in the passenger seat pulled a handgun and shot Eddie in the chest. James had his Derringer already in hand, and his bullet hit the shooter in the forehead. The driver emerged as directed.

"Send an ambulance and a murder investigation unit to Madison and Second Street", was James's command.

Connie and Evelyn witnessed the incident from the window: both were aghast and relieved when James seemed unhurt. They raced to the street.

"Connie, we need you to identify the dead man. Was he the man you saw shooting on the street?"

"Yes, he was."

"We will take a cab."

During the ride, James spoke: "What I wanted to tell you is that Robert, Jr.'s grandfather will be attending the weddings, and he would like Robert, Jr. to know about us before he arrives. Are you alright with that?"

"It is your call, James."

"Do you want to be with me when I tell him? Have you changed your mind?"

"No, you do it. Just let me know when you do."

80

"What are your plans now?" Evelyn asked Jeff.

"I feel good and energetic; perhaps I will look for a job."

"Does law enforcement interest you? I could help if it does."

"I don't think I have the 'balls' to do that work. Pointing a gun at a drug dealer would not be my choice. I don't want to be around drugs, and the first thing I am going to do is move. I met a young woman in rehab, and we plan to date and help each other avoid the drug scene."

"I know an apartment that is available, and I will pay the first three month's rent. You can pay me back when you find a job. A cop who recently got killed on duty had the place. Keep me posted on the job search."

"Evelyn, my pigeons need to be fed. Would you like to go with me?"

"I didn't know you had pigeons: are they at your house?"

"No, they are on the roof of a warehouse."

While they were riding in the cab, Evelyn asked: "May I ask why on the roof of a warehouse?"

"You can ask but I can't answer. Pull over here, cabbie."

They walked two blocks and climbed a two-story fire escape on a building with a painted sign: "MANHATTAN DISCOUNT FUR-NITURE."

Six pigeons were roosting comfortably, and one had a note attached to its leg.

"These pigeons need to be fed daily, and I might ask you to feed them sometimes if I am out of town. Which reminds me; I am going to Atlanta on Saturday and would like you to go along."

"I work at the salon on Saturday."

"Evelyn, since we are getting married next month, I would like you to quit your job. I want you to travel with me."

"I will gladly do that. May I ask why you are going to Atlanta?"

"Just for us to look at some investment property."

Bird with Expanded Wings

After dropping Evelyn off at the salon, James read the pigeon note: "Miami fence mended."

81

Manhattan Community College was more than a little intimidating for Robert, Jr. Connie and Alice were excited to enter the environment. They had decided to become night school students, as well. Alice joined Robert, Jr. as a sociology major, and Connie was majoring in political science.

"Connie, why political science?" Alice asked. "You have never even voted."

"I am frustrated with what I hear on TV. It doesn't make any sense: why can't they understand that automatic weapons are dangerous to society? Why do the lawmakers fight on every issue instead of solving problems? I am going to vote, and I want to understand how the system is supposed to work. What are you going to do with your sociology education?"

"Probably nothing, I just want to help Robert, Jr. meet his goal. He is very excited to be married, us living together, and helping get young people off the streets. His writing skills are very weak, and I can write for him while he learns."

"Is he going to continue playing pool with James?"

"He hasn't said anything, but I think it is good for him. Enjoying his passion will be a relaxing distraction from studying."

"Do you plan on starting a family?"

"We haven't talked about that either, but I would like to wait until he finishes school. Being a new husband, new father, and new college student is a lot to deal with: add to that, finding out that James is his father and meeting his grandfather is a little overwhelming for anyone."

"Yes, I am concerned that he will resent me not telling him about James being his father."

"I think I can help him understand and accept your decision. When is James going to tell him?"

"I don't know, I don't think he has decided yet; however, it will be before your wedding."

82

"Robert, Jr., are you planning on starting a family when you get married?"

"No, Alice wants to wait, and I am not in any hurry. I don't even know how to be a father. Hopefully, studying sociology will help me figure that out."

"When you do, I don't want you to put your life in danger any longer at the pool events. You owe it to your child to be there for him or her. You know what it is like growing up without a father, and you don't want to take that chance. Besides, I would feel terrible if I caused that to happen. I told you that I had been in love only once, but I didn't tell you that I have a son. Never having been able to parent him has been a big regret for me. I made a mistake when I got his mother pregnant. I was young and let my passion overrule my judgment. It is a mistake that I regret every day. His mother and he have had to pay a price for my lack of self –control.

"Are you in contact with him?"

"Only recently have I been able to reach out to him."

"How did he react when you reached out?"

"I haven't had the opportunity to see his reaction yet."

"I have often thought about meeting my father and what I would say to him."

"Robert, Jr., I hope you would listen to what he says before you react. Maybe he had a reason for leaving you. I am hoping that is what my son will do."

"Well, he is probably dead or in prison, and I will never meet him. That is probably best because I don't need him now. I could never forgive him for what he did to my mother. Her heart attack and lonely life have been miserable: lately, she seems to be happier. I think it is because Alice and I are together. I wish she had someone to care for her. I know I have not been a good son: Alice has made me realize that."

"Robert, Jr., you have the rest of your life to be a good son and husband. Remember that every day and make your mother happy. I know someone who might be a candidate to add some light to her life. I hope she will agree to give him a chance. Do you think she might?"

"I don't know but I will suggest it to her before you ask."

"Robert, Jr., in two weeks you will be standing in a Catholic church. Do you have any concern about giving up your total freedom?"

"Not at all: I didn't handle that situation very well. Living alone in a trailer doesn't compare to living with Alice. How about you?"

"I am a little concerned about immersing Evelyn in my lifestyle. Even though she seems comfortable with not understanding my life, she could start to ask questions which I cannot answer. I don't have a real home, and she has never asked me where I live. I move across the country from hotel to hotel. What little personal belongings I have, I keep on a houseboat on the river: that is my place to escape from the ugly world I live in nearly every day. I move the location of the houseboat regularly."

"Don't you think you should tell her how you live?"

"She says she doesn't care, and I won't tell her unless she asks. How do you like college?"

"I haven't decided yet. I am glad Alice is going with me: she explains all the things that I don't understand. Like, why do a couple of students try to dominate the group's discussions? Alice explained it is their psychological need to behave that way. They don't realize they are being annoying, and hopefully, will learn that in one of their classes. Alice has improved my vocabulary, and I am getting more comfortable talking to other students."

"Are the other students friendly?"

"Most of them are. Being in night school, they all have jobs."

"How long will you be going to school?"

"I can earn a certificate in two years if I go three nights per week. Then I can be an intern in a group home for 'at-risk' teenagers."

"Sounds like you are really motivated to that."

"Yes, I think I would like to use my street life experiences to convince kids that it is not a good life."

Bird with Expanded Wings

"It gives me real pleasure to see you pursuing a goal."

83

Freedom Flight

"Fred, are you still motivated to create artistic welding? You seem to be a little frustrated with the industrial welding."

"I am having a difficult time enjoying my efforts. It feels like work rather than pleasure. I would like to create but the mechanics of welding are arduous for me. You are right; it may not be the outlet I thought it would be."

"Do you think you would like to draw your creations on paper?"

"I don't know. I have never tried to draw. I can visualize my intended creation. That is an interesting thought. Let me see what happens. Give me some paper, and I will explore."

"Fred, that is very clear, and I could weld that statue of Joseph fishing just from your drawing. I think we have a business venture evolving from the 'baiting of a hook'. You can draw all the aspects of Joseph's young life as he matures, and I will produce your drawings and his passions in welded art forms. We can name the business: "Capturing the Spirit of Youthfulness". You can draw and do the marketing, and I will be in the back-room welding. Our clients can visit the studio and watch me weld their children's' passions. I think the uniqueness of our venture, coupled with your sales skills, could be very exciting. You won't need any more BMW's. What do you think of the idea?"

"I am overwhelmed! How did you come up with this idea, in an instant or have you been contemplating it?"

"It just came to me now as we were talking: an inspiration from the universe. It surprises me as much as you. I feel euphoric and a bonding with you that exceeds my expectations."

She moved slowly to his athletic frame and put her arms around him to squeeze his solid buttocks. He responded by wrapping his arms around her and squeezing her breasts to his chest. Slowly, he moved his hand to her head and moved it to make her lips accessible. A soft prolonged kiss resulted in both of their tongues wagging with desire inside the other's mouth. He effortlessly picked up her 117 pounds and carried her to his back-yard hammock. She felt his intense emotion as he caressed her breasts while she was moving rhythmically to the comfort of the hammock. She remained the non-participating subject of his desires while he determined every move. His wet tongue tasted every morsel of her big breasts. To her surprise, she felt her nipples harden when he bit each one tastefully. Her mind went limp as she reacted to his tenderness. She only wanted to continue to receive his lovemaking. The complete submission she felt was a first-time experience. There was no doubt: she knew this man cared about her, and not just her body. His lovemaking was too tender and filled with emotion to be just lust. Being completely de-robed in the bright sunlight and sitting on the swaying hammock, she watched as he went to the ground on his knees and kissed her inner thighs ever so tenderly. Then his tongue moved to her clitoris, and he consumed her femininity. She had never permitted a man that pleasure previously. Her sensation raced to her emotional reservoir and, void of expectations, she moaned as her climax generated her serenity.

"Oh, Fred, that was beautiful."

"Joan, I think you already know that I am in love with you. I wanted to wait for this moment to tell you. That was just an appetizer. Now I want to take you to my bed and serve you filet. I hope you like your entrée 'well done'."

<h1 style="text-align:center">84</h1>

"Amanda, how long has it been since you talked to your brother?"

"Probably two years, mother. How's he doing since rehab?"

Amanda's defensiveness had obviously decreased, James concluded, after Eddie's sudden death. Perhaps she realized how life can disappear in a moment.

"He wants to find a job but hasn't decided yet what he wants to do. He has moved out of that drug neighborhood, and James is paying his rent for three months until he finds a job. I would like you and him to visit. I know you always fought like cats and dogs, but it is past time to put that behind you. Life is too short to neglect family. It would be a great wedding present from both of you. Are you still using drugs?"

"I haven't since Eddie was murdered. I am afraid I might stay intoxicated forever. I only knew him a very short time, but it was sobering to see his life end so quickly."

"Have you heard from your father?"

"About three months ago, he called me from prison and said he was sorry about everything. He sounded sincere but he has done that before and then evaporated for a year. Give me Jeff's number, and I will call him."

"Jeff, it's Amanda. How are you?"

"Wow, I haven't heard your voice in some time. Mom must have put you up to it."

"You're right. She bribed me saying this call would be our joint wedding gift, but I am glad she did. Brothers and sisters should talk to each other, regardless of their disagreements. So how are you doing?"

"I feel good since rehab, haven't had any urge to use drugs. I met a woman there, and we both vowed to help each other stay clean. We spend a lot of good time together. How about you? Mom said a cop you were dating got killed by a drug dealer. That must have been tough."

"Well, it did make me realize that anyone's life can end at any moment. The guy who killed Eddie was a drug dealer who may have been supplying my boyfriend, which is a sobering thought."

"My girlfriend is a waitress, and she wants us to open a breakfast and lunch business. James has offered to fund us with a low interest loan. You have been a waitress. Would you like to work with us?"

"I will give that some thought. I would like to meet your new friend.

<h1 style="text-align:center">85</h1>

"Robert, remember you have to write a paper for tomorrow's class. We need to work on it tonight."

"I remember the subject is 'school shootings', and I have mixed feelings about gun control."

"Fine, then write about your mixed feelings. The teacher wants to see how your mind thinks, and hopefully not about your specific opinion."

Robert sat down immediately at the kitchen table in his new apartment and wrote: "What to do to stop school shootings". It seems to me that numerous factors contribute to this problem:

1. Mental illness
2. Lack of satisfactory school security
3. Availability of automatic weapons
4. Lawmakers are unwilling to change the laws

Until all four of these factors can be addressed, the school shootings are unlikely to stop.

"Alice, I have started my paper: let me read it to you. I need your feedback."

"Robert, I think it is terrific. I am impressed with your growing vocabulary. Now you need to expand each factor with more explanation and possible solutions. You are on target to get an 'A'."

Robert did get an "A", and it boosted his confidence to not only pass the course, but to excel.

Alice put a much different slant on her essay. She offered her opinion that arming teachers was a dangerous solution. She felt that teachers, to be effective, should focus only on teaching to the individual student. It was her opinion that teachers being required to baby-sit unruly students reduced their effectiveness. She felt that holstering a gun, acting as a policeman, would only further reduce their objective. She also received an "A".

"Alice, when we finish this two-year program, what do you want to do with this education?"

"I haven't thought about it, I only want you to graduate and do what you want."

"Well, I have been thinking we could open our own shelter and take in kids who are hanging out on the streets, rather than getting an education. Of course, we would need to get it funded. Maybe James could help us find donors, as he seems to have a lot of contacts."

"Sounds like a good idea to me. Let's think on it. We have a lot of time to decide."

"Alice, remember that James and I are playing pool in Atlanta this Saturday."

"Can I go along?"

"I don't know, I will ask James when I see him."

"Yes, Robert, Jr., Evelyn will be going to Atlanta; however, we are flying down on Wednesday as I have business to conduct. She will fly back on Saturday before we play pool. Let's win this one as it will be awhile before we play again, with the wedding and honeymoon the following Saturday. Are you comfortable carrying the Glock for your protection?"

"Yes, but I want to practice shooting this week."

"Good idea."

"Alice, James and Evelyn are going to Atlanta on Wednesday, and she is flying home alone on Saturday."

"Why are they doing that?"

"I am not sure except that James said he was doing some business there. I will fly back on Sunday alone."

"I don't like all this mystery with James. Connie and Evelyn think he is FBI or CIA undercover. Have you seen any evidence of that?"

"No, I think he buys and sells real estate, and wants his investments to be secret. He is probably using his pool winnings to invest, and not using a bank. If he uses different company names to register as the owner, no one knows he has the property. If he put the money in a bank, he would need to pay taxes on the income. I knew a man who was doing that when I was running with the street gang, although I think his money was coming from drugs."

"If he is doing anything illegal, I don't want you involved."

"Alice, all I do is shoot pool and win money, nothing illegal about that."

Robert wasn't comfortable misleading her; however, it was in her best interest he had decided. Winning at pool was very satisfying, and the money provided a comfortable life. He even found the Glock in his ankle holster exciting.

86

Freedom Flight

"Jeffrey, I received an invitation today from my sister in New York. My nephew Robert, Jr. is getting married, and I would like very much to be there. Would you consider going with me? I would enjoy it so much more if you were with me."

"Of course, I will go."

"You need to know something before we go. It has been bothering me for a very long time. Those pictures I sent you of that beautiful woman when you were locked-up:

Jeffrey interrupted: "Jenny, I have forgotten those pictures a long time ago. You should forget it also."

"You will meet the woman in those pictures; she is my sister's best friend and will be getting married in the same ceremony: a double wedding. I didn't want you to freak-out when you saw her."

"That is pretty funny! I am going to the wedding of a woman who I have never met but provided me sexual satisfaction for two years. I guess her husband would not appreciate it as humorous if I told them that story."

"Don't you dare! I would be so embarrassed and devastated. It would reveal an aspect of my life that I am very ashamed of."

"Jenny, even though you intentionally misled me, and I was honestly very surprised when I first met you, this is a case of 'the results justifying the means.' When I review those six terrible years, and the consequence of falling in love with you, I am happy to have paid the price. My life now is so much more fulfilled than before I went to prison. Be at peace with your transgression and take pleasure in providing me a new life."

Once again, Jenny felt the burden of guilt lifting from her shoulders. She also felt blessed that Joan had come into her life and provided her counsel. Otherwise, she would have surely needed to confess to Jeffrey in order to feel healthy within herself. The universe does work in mysterious ways, she concluded.

"Let's drive and do some sightseeing on the way. I have always wanted to visit the City of Rivers and ride the 'incline'. It looks very inviting on TV."

"What city is that?"

"Pittsburgh. The Allegheny and Monongahela rivers meet at a point in downtown to form the Ohio River. The Pirates baseball stadium and the Steelers football stadium sit at that point."

"Sounds nice, I will make a hotel reservation at that point, if I can. Would be nice to view the rivers from the hotel room. Maybe I can hit a home run and catch a touchdown pass while we are in the bedroom!" both chuckled.

87

"Evelyn, our flight leaves at 10 A.M. on Wednesday. I will meet you at 8:00 A.M. at the check-in counter."

"I will be there. Should I bring my new wardrobe?"

"Of course, we are going out on the town Friday night."

"Have you thought about where we are going on our honeymoon?"

"Yes, I thought we would travel on a houseboat down the river and drop anchor when the urge hits us. We can dock at some small towns and explore their bars. Does that sound appealing?"

"Charming, I can have you to myself 24/7. You can drop the boat anchor, and I will raise the 'bird' to new elevations. Your pigeons and the 'bird' on your neck keep us soaring. By the way, who will feed the pigeons while we are house boating?"

"I will send them out of town."

Thursday morning, they were picked up at the hotel by a realtor.

"Hello, Mr. and Mrs. Whitmore."

"Not yet, we get married in eleven days", he responded.

"Just call me Evelyn."

"Are you sure you don't want to look at more than the one home? I have other similar properties."

"No, I am only interested in the one I called you about."

Evelyn thought the property they inspected was not much different than what they had seen in Philadelphia. James told her to ask questions as a prospective buyer. He listened patiently while she addressed everything from room size to drapes, and even was critical of the tile in the master bedroom shower for two.

"This tile needs to be more comfortable and a warm relaxing color", as she smiled at James.

The realtor pretended not to hear her seductive comment.

James responded: "That is an easy fix."

James arrived at Robert, Jr.'s room as scheduled and handed him the Glock.

"It is most likely that you will need this protection tonight. One of our opponents will be the same individual who I believe had us fingered in Chicago. If I am correct, he will be determined to rob us if we win. Are you sure you are up to it?"

"I am sure. Let's win."

James was driving a silver Porsche and to Robert Jr.'s surprise, he drove to the iron gates. "Two-ball in the side pocket", he announced to the gate keeper. They parked as close to the front door as possible, although it was probably fifty yards.

"When we leave the room, I will make it obvious that I am carrying all the money. You go out first, Glock in hand, and drive the car to the front door. This house doesn't have a good escape route. It is unlikely that we will encounter any pursuers until after we drive through the gate. When we do, press the pedal to the floorboard and get on I-75 North. The navigation system is set."

The competition, nine teams, was the best Robert, Jr. had seen. The final "best of three" resulted in a 1-1 tie. The third game break was earned by James, based on his unbeaten record for the evening. If he ran the table, the pot was theirs. James missed his third shot, and it appeared they had lost. However, the pressure may have caused the opponent to miss a difficult 8-ball shot. Robert, Jr. now had a full table length shot with the 8-ball resting against the rail. It required a bank shot to the full table length. With supreme confidence, he "kissed" the 8-ball against the cushion and it slowly traversed the length of the green cloth to the opposite corner and fell in with the last revolution.

"Miraculous shot", James remarked.

Robert, Jr. didn't deem it miraculous as he had practiced it a thousand times, he thought. The opponents only scowled and sat, instead of leaving, as James pocketed the loot.

Robert, Jr. arrived at the car without incident. As he started the car, he noticed a flashing light coming from the trees. It looked to him like a signal. His adrenaline rush was euphoric, rather than generating panic. He drove the Porsche toward the trees, and a bullet pierced the passenger side windshield. He opened the driver side door and rolled to the ground while firing the Glock into the trees.

There was silence, no more shots. He drove to the door and heard more shots. James was standing over a body.

"Floor it! The gate is open."

As they reached the gate, more shots rang out as James fired back with Robert, Jr.'s Glock. At 120 MPH on "Buckhead" streets, Robert, Jr. asked: "Why was the gate open?"

"I have the gate code and remote", James replied.

"Are you alright to drive?"

"Never felt better. I think I found a new passion."

"Forget it; remember what I told you about being a father. We could have both been killed. Right now, you feel invincible, but believe me you are not. 'Billy the Kid' was a myth. No one seems to be following us. Drive the speed limit."

No police sirens were audible. Robert, Jr. surmised that drug dealers did not report shootings.

The navigation system guided them to the Asheville airport, and they dropped the car in a parking lot, riding the van to the terminal. James had cleaned the fingerprints from the Glock with solution he had in the glove compartment. The broken windshield would alert attention quickly, Robert Jr. thought.

"I will call a repair truck to have the windshield replaced. They will have the Porsche out of there before morning, and I will rent a car to drive back to Atlanta tomorrow. I need to clean up this mess. They know what you look like, but they don't know where you live. That was your last pool tournament and mine too, for a long time. When all those dealers there tonight are behind bars or dead, I can continue my operation with a new partner. I know who will be dead soon, if not already: the owner of the house we left with guns blazing. The realtor will not be showing that house tomorrow. The blood stains will be too fresh."

When James rented a car, Robert, Jr. glanced at his credit card and license. They read: James Yun. The address was in Memphis, Tennessee. James handed Robert, Jr. his plane ticket for Sunday afternoon, and said: "I would like to have breakfast with you in my room at 7:00 A.M."

They stopped at a deposit box and James inserted the money gave Robert, Jr. the key and said: "Mail this to yourself. We will pick the money up later. If anything happens to me, you know where it is. Neither of us should be traveling with that much money. Here is $10,000 for pocket change."

It wasn't the bonding experience James had envisioned; nevertheless, based on Robert Jr.'s reaction, they had bonded.

88

"Good morning, Robert, Jr., are you still feeling invincible, or has reality set-in?"

"No reality for me, we got away clean and won the event. I am ready to do it again."

"You can't!"

James wasn't wearing a shirt and he turned his back to Robert, Jr.

"Have you ever seen this birthmark before?'

Robert, Jr. was weak and unable to respond.

"Both of your passions are inherited. Shooting pool and shooting bad guys are in your DNA. I am your uncle, your father's brother. I couldn't tell you until I felt you would understand. Your father and your grandfather have the identical birth marks."

"My father is alive?"

"Yes, and he and your grandfather will be at the wedding. The story I told your mother about me is actually my brother's story. Your father was undercover FBI and had to flee to China before you were born to protect your mother. Your father wants to be a part of your life and is planning to remain in the U.S. after the wedding."

"Does my mother know they are coming?"

"No, I thought it would be best if she just sees him at the wedding. I have told her I want her to meet someone. I don't know how she will react; however, the shock will be muted by the excitement of your wedding: the same for you. Do you agree that my plan is the best case for everyone? There isn't any easy way to do this."

"I don't know. It is too much to absorb."

"Your grandfather is Chinese and lives in Beijing. He was undercover FBI, also, and reported drug money being used to purchase vehicles at his dealership. He had a heart attack three years ago and sold the dealership and retired from the FBI. He and your dad play in pool events throughout China. Your dad will be my new partner when the time is right. I am Robert's half-brother. We have different mothers. Your grandmother was American, and you are one-fourth Chinese heritage. Your grandmother was murdered by drug dealers while they were trying to kill your grandfather. He fled to China with the aid of the FBI. Your father remained in the U.S. and worked with the FBI as your grandfather's contact. After arriving in China, my father married my mother, another American who was teaching English. Your father and I are both one-half Chinese heritage. Mei Lin is your aunt and was a contact for her brother when he was undercover. I do have a son who doesn't know me, just like you and your father. You know him as Mike at the pool hall."

"Mike is my cousin?"

"Yes, and I would like your help to get him out of the gang and into my life. Did you and he get along?"

"OK, I guess."

"Let's eat. You probably have a lot of questions."

"I don't have any appetite, but I do have questions when my mind stops whirling. Can I beat my father at pool?"

"Maybe, it will be a challenge and he won't let you win even though he wants you to."

"Does he still love my mother?"

"Most definitely. He has never been with another woman since leaving her."

89

"Robert, Jr., I phoned Atlanta police this morning, and there has not been any report of a shooting in Buckhead. I am going to the house to see what remains. I expect to be back in Manhattan sometime tomorrow."

Robert, Jr. boarded the plane remaining in complete amazement: even shooting and perhaps killing a bad guy didn't parallel his father being alive. His adrenaline was "off the charts". Before this morning his only family was his mother: now he had a father, a grandfather, an uncle, an aunt and a cousin! The wedding will be much bigger than previously thought. His overriding concern was his mother being surprised by Robert. James had asked his opinion on that plan and he was totally uncertain as to what was best. He thought Alice would be the best person to ask that question. He knew he could trust her to keep the secret.

James drove the rental Ford to Buckhead and met a police paddy wagon and van at the house with the Iron Gate: the gate remained open.

"Looks like a battlefield," one of the officers remarked.

They picked up a body laying at the bottom of the entry steps, and then drove to the woods and found two more bodies.

"Did anyone get away?" James was questioned.

"Could be, there were shots coming from the gate as we drove through. The body by the front door is the house owner. He ordered the robbery attempt. If anyone got away, it is unlikely they were pool players who would know our faces. Drive the van around back. Get the paintings first, and then I will point out the other valuables. Some of it is fake."

The paddy wagon headed for the morgue. James drove to Asheville to pick up the repaired Porsche. The van headed for Richmond where the officer was met by a PENSKE truck driven by Mike. The goods were transferred, and the police van returned to Atlanta. Mike drove to the warehouse.

James stopped by the warehouse and sent a pigeon courier: "Four paintings to hang on fence." He then read a note: "House for sale in Richmond" with the address and realtor's phone number. He drove to a parking garage and put the Porsche in storage. The subway took him just two blocks from the river where he walked to the houseboat at 4:00 A.M.: lifted anchor and motored two miles upriver and dropped the anchor. He was exhausted and would sleep soundly all day.

On Monday evening, he called Evelyn from a pay phone: "Can you travel to Richmond on Wednesday?"

"Of course, can we stay over?"

"I wouldn't have it any other way", he replied. "My bird is starving for your attention, and I don't mean pigeons."

"I know what you mean, and I intend to satisfy the bird's appetite."

Evelyn hung up the phone and realized she was "wet" from the seductive talk.

90

"Alice, my world has turned upside down, and I need to talk to you."

"Certainly, come on over."

Alice surmised that James had told Robert that he was his father. She hoped he was handling it well, but he seemed quite upset on the phone. She knew it might be a long conversation that culminated in relieving his stress. That part she looked forward to as it had become very pleasurable for her as well. The scent of his masculinity was addictive. She was anxiously anticipating her wedding night. Making love for the first time would provide a once in a lifetime adventure for both of them. The thought aroused her desire, and it wouldn't be easy to restrain herself given Robert's shocking news about his father. She deeply wanted to share his news with him in the most intimate way.

"Alice, James is my uncle."

Alice was dumbfounded and reacted with numbness.

"He is my father's brother, well half-brother, and my father is coming to the wedding. Mom doesn't know."

It was just too much for Alice to manage in a single outburst.

"Sit down. I need to breathe. I know that James told your mom that he was Robert, and now he told you he isn't. What is true? Do you believe him?"

"Yes, he gave me all the details, and he has my same birthmark. He told me that my father and grandfather have it, also. What he told mom was actually my father's story, and not his."

"Then, James is Robert's surrogate."

"What does that mean?"

"It means he was substituting for Robert. Why did he do that?"

"He wanted to find out about mom's life and my life and prepare her for my father's arrival."

"When is he planning to tell her?"

"He asked me for my opinion: his plan is to have my father arrive as a surprise at the wedding."

"Robert, that would be a terrible thing to do! It could give her another heart attack. You should tell her. That is what I would want if I were her."

"Will you be with me when I tell her?"

"Of course, if that is what you want."

"Please, you can explain why he misled her much better than I can: the surrogate thing."

"I believe he should arrive earlier to talk to Connie; however, it is probably too late to make that change with the airlines. We need to talk to your mom right now. I will call her to ask if we can visit."

"Hello, Connie. This is Alice. Robert, Jr. and I would like to talk to you. Are you available now?"

"Sure, come on over."

91

"Mom, I have some surprising news, but it is all good so don't get worried. My father is alive."

"I know. James has told me he is your father, but I am still not sure I believe him."

"No, mom, James is my uncle: my father's brother."

"What do you mean?"

"Yes, my father and grandfather are coming to the wedding."

Connie physically collapsed on the couch, and Alice scurried to her side with comfort.

"It is alright, Connie. Everything is fine. It is a shock, I know, but a good shock. James was acting as Robert's surrogate to help you and Robert, Jr. They both have only acted in your best interest. James lied to you in order to help Robert, Jr.: no other motive. The story he told you was actually Robert's story."

Alice wasn't certain how much of what she was saying was being heard. Connie was still in shock, and both Alice and Robert, Jr. were very concerned about her health. Her breathing was irregular, and her face was very white.

"Robert, call 911."

"The ambulance arrived in 10 minutes, and Connie was transported to the hospital. Alice and Robert accompanied her. During the trip, her breathing seemed to become more stable with the help of the oxygen.

"Mom, please don't be alarmed. I am fine with it. Father had to flee the country to protect us. He was an FBI agent: a good guy. James told me that my father still loves you and wants to be part of our lives."

Connie only moved her eyes to fixate on his.

"Your mother is out of shock now, and there has been no further damage to her heart. I want to observe her for another hour, and if there isn't any change you can take her home."

The Doctor's words were received with relief.

"Alice, it is a good thing we didn't go with James's plan."

"Yes, the shock of seeing him unexpectedly could have been tragic."

"I will get a cab to take her home, and will stay with her tonight," Alice replied.

92

"Alice, when is Robert getting to New York?"

"I don't know. Mei Lin probably knows."

"I don't want to see him until the wedding. Any conversation with him would detract from the excitement of both weddings. I want him to walk me down the aisle, just as if we had been together for the past twenty-two years."

"Have you picked out your dress?"

"Yes, but I am going to change my selection now."

"Does that mean you're feeling OK about Robert being in your life again?"

"I am feeling OK about his being in Robert, Jr.'s life. I have many questions to discuss with him before I decide how I feel. There have been too many lies. Robert, Jr. seems to have accepted all of it without a problem. He knows James much better than I do. How do you feel about it?"

"It seems to me that their motives were pure; however, there methods are troubling. I was taught that lying is a sin, and I still feel that way. If it were me deciding, I would have Robert come to you and not use James as a surrogate. Although, it did work well with Robert, Jr. He seems to have bonded very well with James. When he talks about him, he always exhibits respect and admiration. Had he met Robert initially, he might not have been as accepting. You should try to get some sleep now. We have some big days coming up. I will be here if you need me."

"That isn't necessary. You can go home."

"I won't hear of it: I couldn't sleep as I would be wondering if you are alright. I can sleep on the couch without being anxious about you: good night!"

93

Freedom Flight

"Connie, this is my friend Jeffrey".

"Jenny, I think you are under-selling him by calling him a friend: And this is Alice, Robert Jr.'s fiancée."

After exchanging introductions and greetings, they sat in Connie's living room and caught up on their lives. Connie explained how Alice and Robert, Jr. met. She revealed that the three of them were going to college, and that Robert, Jr. was no longer living the gang life. She told them about his goal of helping to get teenagers off the street, and into a productive track of life. Jenny could see that her sister's life had finally become happy.

"Jenny, there is one other piece of startling news to tell you. A man appeared out of nowhere and claimed to be Robert, Jr.'s father. His name is James."

She related the details including "Bird with Expanded Wings" and the large check.

"Connie, that is bizarre! How do you feel about all of it?"

Silently, Jenny was amazed that both of them had received a large amount of money despite growing up in poverty. How ironic!

"I am still numb. James is the man who is marrying Evelyn, and I am happy for them."

"Does Robert, Jr. know?"

"Yes, he is fine with meeting his father, and he likes his uncle."

Jeffrey just listened with amazement. He thought he and Jenny's lives evolved with spiritual direction: now her sister's life was even more astonishing.

"The wedding is only two days away, and I have been weighing all this for six months. I guess I can wait until the wedding euphoria has passed to decide how I feel. James gets total credit for resurrecting Robert, Jr.'s life. I can only praise him for that. The grief Robert gave me as a teen-ager has long since evaporated. Jeffrey, Jenny told me that you have written a book about the lives of persons' who have returned to society after being in prison. Are you close to finishing it?"

"I am finished, and the publisher has sent me a contract. I don't know if it is a fair contract, and I guess I will need to hire an agent to evaluate and negotiate for me."

"Where is the publisher located?"

"Here in New York."

"I have a customer at the dress shop that makes her living as an authors' agent. I could ask her to take a look at your story. She is very friendly and nice. She might want to represent you. Did you bring a copy with you?"

"I sure did. It goes with me constantly. In fact, I feel withdrawal if I don't work on it every day. Could I meet her before we leave New York?"

"I will call her. In fact, she asked me if I could invite her to Alice's wedding, and she will be attending."

94

Freedom Flight

"Jenny, your sister's family has made me feel very comfortable. I have never experienced a family togetherness. It is very heartwarming to see all of you enjoying each other's lives and adventure stories. I would like to be a part of your family. Would you consider moving to New York, as my wife?"

"Jeffrey are you proposing marriage?"

"Well, I guess so. A wife needs to be married."

"Oh, my goodness, yes! I never even thought about being a bride. When do you want to take the vows?"

"Tomorrow. We won't tell anyone. I don't want to interfere with their celebration. When we get back to Chicago, we can make it legal. Their wedding reception will be ours also without them knowing it. I will really be a part of your family, even if our ceremony is only symbolic for now."

"What a very romantic plan! I had no idea you could be so impulsive."

"I didn't either, Jenny, but I've never felt more sure about anything. Let's go buy a ring."

95

"Connie, Robert, Jr. received a check today for $360,000 from an off-shore bank made out to an account opened in the name of an enterprise labeled 'Restoring Young Lives'. Who is aware of his interest in pursuing that objective? Someone that is financially well-off?"

"The only possible person that I can think of is his grandfather."

"But why would he be an anonymous benefactor? I would think he would want Robert, Jr. to know that he was supporting his interest."

"Yes, Alice, I would expect that, also. Perhaps it will remain a mystery. The universe never ceases to provide surprises.

96

As they arrived at the Catholic Church, it was obvious that two plain clothes officers were standing outside the door and two more in uniform were seen on the street. Mei Lin was sitting with Suh Yun, her brother. Jeff brought his girlfriend Peggy, and they sat with Amanda. Another six individuals were staged to walk down the aisle: Robert, Jr. and Alice would follow James and Evelyn. The third couple were still staring at each other, not having spoken a word. Robert and Connie would be first to enter the procession. He took Connie's right arm and slowly walked the length of the church aisle. Robert spoke while walking: "You look beautiful, just as I remember. It is very gratifying that both of us get to see our son get married."

Connie didn't acknowledge his words. He felt her uneasiness.

James and Evelyn were embracing with arms wrapped around each other's waist as they walked. They looked as if their lust had never been consummated.

"Evelyn, now I am going to totally share my life with you. We can lie in the same bed _every_ night."

Evelyn squeezed his arm and said: "I so want that. I want all of you, all the time."

Robert, Jr. and Alice did feel like two virgins about to embark on a new adventure.

"Robert, will you be gentle tonight? I know how much you have wanted this day to arrive for what seems like an eternity. Now there will be no more waiting. My dreams about tonight are beautiful and would like it to be just like I have fantasized."

"It will be just as you want for the remainder of our lives. I treasure your willingness to pleasure me these past months, and I intend to focus on your pleasure tonight and forever."

97

The after-wedding party with catered food, including egg rolls and fortune cookies, was attended by 44 law enforcement officers and their spouses. Everyone but James was surprised by their presence. He had arranged for the larger two rooms in the banquet hall and the extra food. Even Alice enjoyed the egg rolls. Her fortune cookie read: "Go forth in new flight."

The reunion of new family members was exhilarating for all. The one-on-one conversations, as well as group discussions, revealed the unknown details of all their lives. Robert, Jr. wanted to corral his father; however, thought it was best to wait as he was one-on-one with Connie. Amanda, Jeff and Peggy took the opportunity to plan their new adventure. James wished that Mike could have attended to meet his unknown family.

"Connie, I am unable to offer any further explanations that you haven't already heard from James. I would like to answer all the questions you must still have."

"James told me that you were in love when we got pregnant. Is that true?"

"One hundred percent true. I have never loved anyone else, before or after you. I always knew that someday I would be able to see you again. The feeling was so strong that my belief was never doubted. I know you didn't have that assurance and your grief never left my mind. To ease my grief, I asked the universe nearly every day to provide you happiness. Until James located you eight months ago, I could only wonder about your life and your recovery from my disappearance. It was selfish of me to solicit your love when I was living a dangerous life. Now that Robert, Jr. has found Alice, I will do everything I can to prevent him from re-entering the gangster life."

"Are you going to remain in the U.S.?"

"Yes, I want to be near my son and his family."

"Did you graduate from college before joining the FBI?"

"Yes, I went to DePaul University in Chicago."

"What about your mother?"

"She was murdered by a drug dealer who was after my dad."

"What are you going to do now?"

"Probably sell cars. It is my only experience other than under-cover law and playing pool."

"Where are you going to live?"

Robert hesitated and then replied softly: "Someday I hope to live above a Chinese dry-cleaning shop."

Connie felt weak and after a long silence, she spoke: "If that is your desire after twenty-two years, I think we need to fulfill my fantasy."

"What is that?"

"For many years, I saw myself jumping into your arms and feeling that bird on your neck."

He took her hand and slowly raised it to his lips and then to the back of his neck.

"I hope my bird can still give you flight."

"All I need is your love: the love I felt when we created Robert, Jr."

They hailed a cab to the Hilton where James had reserved six suites.

"Evelyn, do you think we should invite Jeff and Peggy to stay over in Robert's suite? I don't think he'll be using it."

"I am sure they would appreciate the offer but that leaves Amanda going home alone."

"I can have one of the hall guards escort her. Are their café plans still developing?"

"I'm not sure. Why don't you ask when you offer the suite?"

"I will. Remind me to mail some checks tomorrow."

"What checks?"

"More secrets, Evelyn", and he put the checks in his jacket pocket:

     1. "Police Widow's Charity"

     2. "College Fund for Children of Slain Law Enforcement Officers"

     3. "Chinese Orphans Foundation"

Bird with Expanded Wings

Each check was in the amount of $1,000,000.00.

"Grandfather, will you tell me about your life? James told my mother and me different stories. I don't know what is true."

"Robert, Jr., the truth is I did work for the FBI in Chicago as an undercover agent. Your grandmother was murdered by a drug dealer who was targeting me. The FBI moved me to Beijing and set me up with a new car dealership to identify money launderers. Robert was in grade school when this occurred, and he stayed in the U.S. in a boarding school. He joined the FBI after college graduation. They changed his identity from Robert Yun to Robert Young. He had to flee the country as I did."

"Did you play in pool events with my father in China? Did you make a lot of money?"

"We did alright."

"Are you going to visit Mike before you return to China?"

"Mike who?"

"James's son."

"James doesn't have a son."

"Did you pay your taxes when you lived in the U.S.?"

"Of course, James just made that up to make a good story. He needed to get your mother's attention."

"Does my uncle work for the FBI?"

"No, he manages a secret society of law enforcement officers. They label themselves as the 'Police Widow's Charity'. Don't ever tell him or anyone that I told you. I want you to know he is doing good work. But it must remain a secret."

Robert felt a very strong urge to be part of his uncle's society.

"Here, your aunt said you would like this as a wedding gift."

Robert, Jr. opened an envelope and found two round trip tickets to the Philippines.

"Robert, Jr., James told me about what happened in Atlanta. You were very brave, a natural law man. Getting married means, you must cease playing pool events. It is too dangerous. Your family could be harmed just like your grandmother. It is your responsibility to break the cycle: no pool events and no law-enforcement involvement. Get your education and get kids off the streets. That would make me very happy. Now I must take Mei Lin home. I am sure she is tired."

"I thought she had a room at the hotel."

"Yes, but she prefers to sleep at home. One of the officers will take us."

The hallway guard escorted Suh Yun and Mei Lin to her apartment.

"See you in the morning, sis."

"Good night Suh Yun: you go to hotel: Birds with like feathers should roost together."

Sequel in Progress